PRAISE FOR

THE KNIVES
BEFORE
CHRISTMAS

"A surfeit of Santas seriously complicates a murder investigation... A magical mystery with a Christmas theme."
—KIRKUS REVIEWS

"Holloway sets the tone from the very first sentence. This is going to be a great, fun ride. His characters are unique and imaginatively drawn. And he manages to mix humor, heart and a lot of Christmas spirit into a very satisfying whodunit. It's everything you could possibly want from a light mystery."
—HY CONRAD, head writer for USA Network's *Monk* and author of *Mr. Monk and the New Lieutenant*

"Hidden secrets are everywhere in Holloway's *The Knives Before Christmas*. It's a twisty mystery wrapped up in holiday paper with a magical bow."
—HEATHER WEIDNER, author of the Pearly Girls Mysteries and the Mermaid Bay Christmas Shoppe Mysteries

"A disgruntled and mischievous elf, magic pockets, a self-cleaning house with a guard-alligator, and ho-ho-homicide in the town of Christmas, Florida, where Santas-in-training need to watch their backs... J. Kent Holloway's *Knives Before Christmas* is an imaginative, clever, holly jolly suspenseful time! I highly recommend!"
—MICHELLE BENNINGTON, author of the Hazardous Hoarding series

"A gift! J. Kent Holloway earns himself a prominent place on the 'nice' list with this wonderful tale. In *The Knives Before Christmas*, Holloway grafts a solid traditional mystery onto the legend of Santa Claus, with delightful results... Fans of cozies and Christmas mysteries will want Santa to bring this one to their house!"

—**NIKKI KNIGHT**, author of the Grace the Hit Mom Mysteries

"When there's a murder in Christmas, Florida, who better to solve the crime than the guy who's next in line to become the real-life Santa Claus? And of course Santa's helpers—a sentient house, a persnickety elf, and a thirteen-foot guard alligator. Do they get the job done? Ho, ho, ho! *The Knives Before Christmas* is a droll delight!"

—**MOLLY MACRAE**, author of the Haunted Shell Shop Mysteries, the Highland Bookshop Mysteries, and the Haunted Yarn Shop Mysteries

THE KNIVES
BEFORE
CHRISTMAS

ALSO BY J. KENT HOLLOWAY

FICTION

The Vampire's Valet

The Curse of One-Eyed Jack

The Legend of the Winterking

Night of the Toad King

Tombstone Voodoo

Haunted Melody

THE GRAND AVENUE DETECTIVES MYSTERIES

The Mystery of the Dying Man

THE EZEKIEL CRANE NOVELS

Curse of the Devil's Teeth

Dirge of the Witch Haints

Feast of the Sin Eater

THE AJAX CLEAN FORENSIC THRILLERS

Clean Exit

RISE OF THE KNIGHT SHADES

Rise of the Knight Shades Book One: The Djinn

THE GRIM DAYS MYSTERIES

Death Warmed Over

Dead in the Water

THE CAPTAIN JOE MYSTERIES

Murder on Voodoo Island

Killypso Island

THE ENIGMA DETECTIVE

Primal Thirst

Siren's Song

Devil's Child

THE JACK SIGLER CONTINUUM NOVELLAS

Guardian

Patriot

Centurion

NONFICTION

I Died Swallowing a Goldfish and Other Life Lessons from the Morgue

THE KNIVES
BEFORE
CHRISTMAS

A SANTA-IN-TRAINING
MYSTERY

KEYLIGHT
B O O K S
AN IMPRINT
OF TURNER
PUBLISHING

J. KENT HOLLOWAY

KEYLIGHT BOOKS
AN IMPRINT OF TURNER PUBLISHING COMPANY
Nashville, Tennessee
www.turnerpublishing.com

The Knives Before Christmas
Copyright © 2025 by J. Kent Holloway. All rights reserved.

This book or any part thereof may not be reproduced or transmitted in any form or by any means, electronic or mechanical, including photocopying, recording, or by any information storage and retrieval system, without permission in writing from the publisher.

This is a work of fiction. All the characters and events portrayed in this book are either products of the author's imagination or are used fictitiously.

Cover design by J. Kent Holloway
Cover art by M. Wayne Miller, www.mwaynemiller.com
Book design by William Ruoto

Library of Congress Cataloging-in-Publication Data
Names: Holloway, J. Kent, author.
Title: The knives before Christmas / J. Kent Holloway.
Description: Nashville, Tennessee: Turner Publishing Company, 2025.
Identifiers: LCCN 2024048567 (print) | LCCN 2024048568 (ebook) |
ISBN 9798887980706 (paperback) | ISBN 9798887980713 (hardcover) |
ISBN 9798887980720 (epub)
Subjects: LCGFT: Cozy mysteries. | Christmas fiction. | Novels.
Classification: LCC PS3608.O49414 K65 2025 (print) | LCC PS3608.
O49414 (ebook) | DDC 813/.6—dc23/eng/20250307
LC record available at https://lccn.loc.gov/2024048567
LC ebook record available at https://lccn.loc.gov/2024048568

Printed in the United States of America

For my Mom and Dad, who (despite their utter chagrin)

never made me stop believing in Santa Claus, and in fact

enabled my man-child sense of wonder.

THE KNIVES BEFORE CHRISTMAS

1

Santa Claus lying dead at my feet was the last thing I wanted to stumble over the moment I walked into my shop. After the evening I had last night, filled with screaming kids, irate parents, and near-homicidal Christmas shoppers, I'd hoped today would be an improvement. I should have known better, because when I turned the key and opened the door, I knew with little doubt that today was going to be much worse.

The dead department-store Santa was proof of that.

Catching my breath at the surprise corpse, I stepped back out of my store's front door and glanced at the number etched above the entrance: *334.* My eyes drifted up to the unlit sign hanging from my covered porch roof, just above the door bearing a Victorian-style neon script in green and yellow that spelled out *Wonderland* with festive loops and swirls.

Yep. This is my store all right.

334 Comet Avenue, Christmas, Florida.

The large Queen Anne-style Victorian home that housed my holiday-themed shop had been my place of employment for the past twenty-two years now, I suppose. I'd owned it for the last six. Ever since Horatio Longpepper, the last Santa-in-Training, had passed away and bequeathed the place to the next person in line.

Yes, that would be me.

I'd taken up residence in the third-floor turret, just as Horatio had, and left the first two floors for the store where it was Christmas 364 days a year.

Pushing past the memories, my curiosity welled. I stepped back into the showroom and bent down for a closer look at the imposter Santa. His suit, speckled with dirt and grime, had seen better days. But the filth wasn't the only blemish on his suit. Several splotches of red, the unmistakable color of drying blood, dotted his back; they were a much darker shade than the rest of the outfit. I counted at least eleven such blood stains encircling narrow slits in the fabric—telltale signs of stab wounds.

Before you get the wrong impression of me, I'm not Sherlock Holmes, not by a long shot. I'm not hyper-observant or super-deductive or anything like that. The only reason I suspected they were stab wounds was because of the knife lying next to the body, an old-fashioned Swiss Army knife with an image of a Christmas tree on the handle where the Swiss cross normally would sit. The blade was covered in blood.

If the Christmas-tree ornamentation hadn't given it away already, I instantly recognized the knife. It matched one of six identical pocketknives I'd given out over fifteen years ago to a handful of my closest friends and best Santa customers. One of them had since passed away. Four were still alive and Santa-ing around. And the fifth—well, let's just say he fell on some pretty hard times, and leave it at that. Either way, I suppose, they would all soon be considered suspects in a murder investigation.

Hmmmm. Oh, how keen.

I'd just realized that *I* was probably going to be a suspect too. After all, the knives had come out of my own workshop. The dead guy was in my store. And, as far as I knew, I had no one to corroborate my whereabouts last night after leaving the Santa gig in Orlando, other than the hotel front-desk guy, who had seemed far more interested in his smartphone than who came or went from his establishment.

Maybe they have cameras in the lobby? I thought. *Of course, with my luck, they'd be on the fritz.*

After a moment, I realized that my concerns were bordering on the macabre. As I've already stated, I was no detective and had no business being this close to a dead body...especially as a potential suspect in my own shop. I stood and gave the body one more look-over.

Though the knife and the Santa suit were beckoning to me like a sugar-plum fairy to an all-you-can-eat candy buffet, I knew better than to roll him over for a better peek at his face. The cops wouldn't look too kindly on my doing anything more than checking for a pulse—which I'd already done.

But I knew most of the Santas in the area. If you were a professional or semi-professional Santa, or just enjoyed dressing up in red-velvet long johns, chances are you'd been to my shop. It was the premier spot for everyone's Christmas and Santa-related needs in the region. And because most pro Santas frequented my store, there was a better-than-good chance that I knew the corpse who was making like rigor mortis on my hardwood floors.

I needed to at least see the dead Santa's face, sans the discount white nylon beard.

Slowly, I reached toward the body. My hand hovered over his left shoulder as I contemplated my admittedly shoddy wisdom. Fortunately, sanity soon won out over complete stupidity, and I backed away while taking a deep breath.

The cops were already going to read me the riot act for hovering over the body for so long. My time would be best suited to—

Crap. Cops!

I hadn't even called 911 yet. I reached into the spacious pocket of my suit jacket—the green one with bright red pinstripes—and pulled out my cell phone. A moment later, I was speaking with police dispatch, reporting my discovery. Having seen enough cop shows in my life to know what they'd want me to do, I stepped out my door while I was still on the phone with them and closed it behind me. Ten minutes later, a cruiser, blue and red lights flashing brighter than the morning sun, whipped into the parking lot with its tires squealing. Two uniformed Orange County deputies—one older and more world-weary, the other little more than a kid by my reckoning, with eager, excited eyes—climbed out and dashed across the stone walkway leading from the lot to the shop's entrance. As they approached, the older deputy, obviously winded, nearly doubled over as he tried to catch his breath. His partner beat him to me with minimal effort.

"You're the complainant?" he asked, his voice high-pitched. I couldn't tell if it was from excitement, or if he hadn't quite hit puberty yet.

I nodded in reply. "Thomas Nast," I said, extending my hand in greeting. He looked at it like it carried the bubonic plague or something, and I realized that, in his eyes, I was already a suspect.

You should understand something about the town in which I live. Christmas can hardly be considered a town. Besides my little holiday shop, it's got a post office, a handful of historical sites, the world's largest alligator-shaped building, and a population of a little over fifteen hundred people. It's basically a stop-sign attraction on the way to Disney World, where people drive out of their way just to mail letters to themselves for the Christmas postmark they'll receive when they get home from their vacation.

It's not incorporated and doesn't have its own police or fire department. For those services, residents of Christmas rely on

Orange County and its Sheriff's Office for all its crime-related needs. And since crime in Orlando is considerably more brutal and more frequent than it is here, the deputies who visit us bring their own suspicions and worries with them...and act as though they're fish in a barrel just waiting to get popped. Every set of eyes is targeting them. Every pair of hands is a deadly weapon, waiting to take their lives. Mostly, they're not quite aware of how things work in our smaller, quieter neck of the woods, and it shows when they arrive to any call they get here. It's a bit of contention among the community that the moment the cops show up to anything—even something as innocuous as a loud-music complaint—the citizens of Christmas, who typically are among the lower middle class on the socioeconomic scale, are instantly treated like criminals.

To ease the young deputy's tension, I gave him my best Santa Claus smile, then thought better of it since there was a dead guy a few hundred feet behind me. Respect for the dead dictates that smiles should not be shared by anyone within such proximity. Especially anyone who may or may not be considered a suspect.

He opened his mouth to say something else, when two more patrol cars pulled into the lot, and the older deputy stepped up to take over the interview. He instructed the newcomers to clear the scene and secure it, and advised the junior deputy that he would talk to me about what had happened. The younger partner seemed thrilled at the prospect, and he and the two other responding deputies strode carefully into my shop with guns drawn.

"So," the older guy said. The name plate above his shirt pocket said his name was Rockfeld. "You called this in?"

I nodded, repeated my name, then explained what I had found when I came to work this morning. He jotted everything down, his eyes squinting and lips pursed like he was having trouble seeing the little notebook in his hand. Reaching my hand in my coat pocket, my fingers fumbled around inside.

"Need reading glasses?" I asked.

He rolled his eyes with a nod. "Stupid me left them at roll call this morning. Guess I'm going to have to run to a store later today to buy a new pair."

"What are you? A 1.50 or a 2?" I asked, inquiring about the grade of reading glasses he used.

He shrugged. "Actually, a 2.50," he said. "These old eyes ain't what they used to be."

I cast him an understanding smile, then continued my tactile search of my pocket until I found what I was looking for. A moment later, I whipped out a brand-new pair of glasses and offered them to the deputy.

One of his eyebrows arched curiously. "You just happened to have a pair of 2.50s in your jacket?"

"I played Santa last night," I said. "Covered for a friend of mine. He's sick. The glasses were left in his dressing room, and I grabbed them to return to him when he's feeling better."

It was true that I'd covered for a sick friend last night. The bit about the glasses was a complete lie, but I couldn't very well tell him the truth about my suit and its unusual properties. Besides, I figured Santa would forgive me the falsehood if it helped the aging deputy to see better.

Rockfeld held the glasses up to his nose with a nod of thanks, then slipped them on and continued jotting down notes of everything I'd told him. After I'd given him my demographics, I recounted the fact that I'd left Wonderland yesterday around three thirty in the afternoon to help my sick friend out, leaving the store in the care of the manager, Tricia "Trixie" McNamara, who would have locked up around five. No, I hadn't spoken to her since then. No, I did not know who the dead Santa in my shop was. No, I couldn't imagine Trixie having anything to do with the death. She didn't have a violent bone in her body, and I trusted her completely.

"Does your place have an alarm system?" Deputy Rockfeld asked. "Was it armed?"

I shook my head. "It has one, but it hasn't been armed in years." I shrugged. "I don't even think we have a monitoring service anymore. At least I haven't paid any dues as far back as I can remember."

He scribbled that down. "So, was the store locked up tight when you got here?"

"Yeah, I remember having to fidget with the door to get the lock to pop," I said, then bit down on my tongue. I shouldn't have told him that, but it slipped out before I had thought it through. The thing you'll learn about my House—my store—is that it, like my suit...is kind of special. Doesn't matter if someone forgot to lock the doors. The House would automatically take care of it for us. Therefore, I don't know for sure if a killer locked the place up after they left or if the House did it for them. But I couldn't exactly explain that to the cops, now, could I?

"Who all has keys to the place?"

I told him that myself and Trixie were the only ones with keys.

The questions went on like this for several minutes, until Deputy Rockfeld seemed satisfied. He closed his notebook before stuffing it into his shirt pocket.

"All right, Mr. Nast." I watched as the door to my shop opened and the three younger deputies stepped out, securing yellow crime-scene tape along the covered wrap-around porch of the business. "We've got Major Crimes detectives on their way. They'll want to talk to you, so you'll need to stick around."

"Sure." I glanced over at the first deputy I'd spoken to. His nameplate read *Jenkins*. "Any idea who he is?" I asked him, as he took the two steps leading down from the porch. "Or how he got inside my store?"

"I'm sorry, sir," he said. "Can't really discuss the case right now. Active investigation and all that."

I nodded my understanding and walked over to my Christmas-red 1957 Ford Thunderbird—being Florida, I had the great fortune to have driven to work that morning with its top down—and leaned against a tail fin to wait for the detectives.

As I watched the deputies continue about their business, my mind raced, wondering about the dead man inside. Who is he? And how had he ended up in my store? At the moment, the only things I knew for sure were that he was as dead as a Christmas tree in April, and that one of my custom-made pocketknives was most likely the murder weapon.

But that still left the question: How had he ended up in Wonderland to begin with? Had Trixie let him in and left?

Trixie.

I withdrew my watch from the pocket of my vest and checked the time. It was a few minutes before eight thirty. She should have been here by now. During the Christmas season, the store opened at nine, and part of her job duties as manager was to get here early to set up the displays and do a quick inventory of the stock.

Pulling out my phone, I flipped through my contacts until I found hers and pressed the call button. The other end rang a few times, then went to voicemail. I hung up, concerned. It wasn't like Trix to be late. And although she preferred texting to talking on the phone, like most twenty-one-year-olds these days, she never hesitated to answer when she saw it was me calling.

The sound of gravel crunching had me wheeling around to see an old Chevy pickup pulling into the parking lot, George Trabor's face gawking from behind the steering wheel at the police cars as he coasted up next to my T-Bird. As he drew closer, he rolled down his window and let out a low whistle.

"Looks like you've had some trouble." He shifted the truck into neutral and watched as the deputies searched the perimeter of the store. "What's going on, Tom?"

George was one of my more frequent customers. He'd been playing Santa for the kids at the YMCA for the last thirty years, and had been Horatio Longpepper's best friend since they were kids. When talking to customers, Horatio would often tell them it was George who'd persuaded him to start Wonderland in the first place, but that was just as much a fib as my little white lie to Deputy Rockfeld about the reading glasses. Like me, Horatio had his own, more secret agenda for running this crazy Christmas store, but he liked to credit George for it nonetheless. It was, after all, more believable than the truth.

George was also one of the six men I'd given a knife to, but now was not the time to ask him anything about it.

I shrugged. "Not really sure what happened," I told him. "Came to work and found a dead guy in the store's atrium." I was hesitant to tell him too much. Not that I didn't trust him or even thought he might be a cold-blooded murderer or anything. But he *was* a bit of a gossip, and the last thing we needed was for the rumor mill to start whispering about murder in our little town.

"That's not something one finds every day, I reckon."

I gave him a sad smile and shook my head. "Nope. Thank goodness."

"Who is it?"

"Huh?"

"The stiff. Who's the dead guy?"

"No idea. He was face down on the floor, dressed in a Santa suit—beard and all. Couldn't get a good look at him."

George turned his attention back to the deputies. "Was he murdered?" he asked me while tamping down the tobacco in the bulb of his pipe and lighting it.

I winced at the question and proceeded with caution. "Not really sure." It was the truth. I suppose the guy could have stabbed himself in the back. If he was really limber. And had four-foot-long arms. "I didn't really pay much attention. I was too busy processing what I was seeing; then I called the police."

Tact. It can be beneficial when push comes to shove, and I hoped it would belay any rumors that might start spreading. I wasn't worried about the business's reputation or anything. But the last thing Christmas needed was a fearful mob thinking they might be next on some crazy killer's personal hit list. Don't laugh. Nuttier things have been believed among the citizens of Christmas, Florida.

George nodded at my explanation but remained silent for the next several minutes, as if in deep thought. Then he turned back to me after he seemed to have gotten enough of the excitement. "Any idea when you'll be opening today?" he asked. "I need a few things before my gig tonight."

"I honestly can't say. It depends on how long the police take to do their thing."

As I was saying this, another vehicle pulled up into the parking lot. A late-model Ford Taurus. Although it was unmarked, it screamed of being a detective's car.

When George noticed it, he gave me a wave. "Well, looks like you're about to have some more visitors. Call me when you can open."

"If it gets too late, I'll call you and you can tell me what you need. I'll try to get it for you."

George chuckled and nodded toward my coat. "You probably got the entire inventory in those crazy pockets of yours."

I laughed. My pin-striped suit with its "miraculous pockets," as my regulars called them, was often the topic of debate around here. I'd told everyone it was an old magician's trick I'd learned from Horatio, which seemed to quell any deep scrutiny from most people.

Satisfied with his joke, George put his truck in gear and drove off just as a rather large, muscular man in a polo shirt and khakis and a blond woman with a detective's shield pinned to her belt walked up to me.

The male detective spoke first after, surprisingly, shaking my hand. "I'm Detective Tice," he said in a deep baritone, then nodded to his partner. "This is Detective Lassiter. I'm assuming you're…" He glanced down at an open notepad. "Thomas Nest?"

"Nast," I corrected. "Thomas Nast."

He nodded, jotting the information down. "Deputy Rockfeld filled me in over the phone on the drive over here," he said, looking past my shoulder as a large Crime Scene unit pulled into the parking lot. "I've got some questions for you, but first we need to look at the scene real quick. Once we've given it a good once-over, either Detective Lassiter or I will come out and interview you."

I watched them walk away and rendezvous with Rockfeld and the Crime Scene crew, no doubt discussing how best to proceed with their investigation. I was getting antsy. The longer this took, the more worried I became about what had happened in my store last night. The fact that Trixie still hadn't showed up to work made me doubly anxious.

Fortunately, I knew someone irrevocably connected to the grand old house who would have more than likely seen everything. He'd be able to tell me exactly what had happened. That is, if I could get him to cooperate.

"Pep, you there?" I'd turned around to avoid being seen by the police as I muttered the words in a hushed tone. It wouldn't be good, after all, to have the cops think I was a lunatic while they were conducting a homicide investigation. "Peppermint? Come on, man. Where are you?"

I waited a good ten heartbeats with no reply.

"This isn't for me," I whispered. "It's for Trixie. I'm worried about her."

"Worried about her? Why?" came a velvety English-accented voice from the back seat of my car.

I squinted at the sound but couldn't see anyone there.

But that's the kind of thing you can expect when dealing with an elf.

2

Horatio had called the elf, whose elfin name was Minlytryasan, Peppermint for two reasons. First, his elfin name was way too hard to pronounce. Most elf names are. Horatio had chosen Peppermint as a *nom de guerre*, a play on words to his own last name, Longpepper. It was sort of his version of Dr. Evil's Mini-Me from the Austin Powers movies.

Peppermint had loved Horatio a great deal. He'd been steadfast to his master and had served him well for over fifty years. When my old mentor had died six years earlier, I'd inherited not only the store he'd lovingly built over the decades, but also the elf who had been bound to the House it was contained in. Unfortunately, Peppermint hadn't been particularly pleased with that little development, and we'd been at odds ever since.

Oh, yeah. I have an elf servant. Guess I should have mentioned that first.

"I need your help, Peppermint," I said, bending over the driver's-side door as if I were searching for something inside the vehicle.

"Why are you worried about Trixie?" he asked again. I still couldn't get past his highbrow English accent. The elf had lived in the Americas since before the white man settled here. He and his people had been revered by the Seminole as the *este lopocke*, their version of the "Little People." As far as I knew, he'd never set foot in the British Isles, and yet he insisted on using this ridiculous accent anyway.

"Because there's a dead guy in our atrium and Trix hasn't shown up for work yet."

There was a long silence after that, and I squinted again, wondering if he'd vanished without offering any assistance whatsoever.

Something you should know about elves. They're not at all what you think of when you imagine Santa's elves. They are not what you think of when imagining Tolkien's elves from *Lord of the Rings* either. Elves are infinitely more complicated than that.

First and foremost, they're spirits. They've got no physical bodies of their own, and the only way you can see them is if: 1) they want you to, 2) you look at them in a certain kind of light, and 3) you stare at them directly front and center. If you try to see them in profile or from behind, forget it. It won't happen. If they turn around on you, they'll disappear. So, outside in the bright sunlight of a December morning in Florida, I could forget any possibility of laying eyes on the pointy-eared little weasel. The only way I was going to know whether he was still with me or not was if he communicated. Given his penchant for driving me up the wall, chances were he was going to let me keep wondering whether he was there or not.

My only hope was Trix. He had a soft spot for the girl. But then we all did.

"Pep, buddy? You still there?" I glanced over my shoulder, but the cops had already entered Wonderland. They weren't paying any attention to me, which was a good thing.

"Did you know there's a dead man in your shop?" Peppermint finally said, making me jump.

"Peppermint! We're talking about Trixie now."

"But the dead man is infinitely more interesting. He seems to be bleeding out all over your hardwood floors."

"Pep!"

Another pause, then: "Why do you not just call Trixie? I'm sure she is perfectly fine."

"I tried. She's not answering." I sighed, checking my watch again. It was now almost nine thirty. It wasn't like her to fail to call to tell me she was going to be late. "So, what happened last night?"

"What do you mean?"

I gritted my teeth, trying to maintain patience for the little imp. Getting upset with him was only going to make things worse, which was exactly why he was goading me right now.

"The dead guy you keep telling me about. What happened to him?"

"Well, my first guess is that he died somehow. Maybe something to do with all those stab wounds in his back."

I pinched the bridge of my nose and stifled a growl. "Pep?"

"How on Earth would I know what happened to him?"

The growl slipped past my defenses, and I narrowed my eyes at the back seat.

"Because, genius, you're a *house* elf. Bound to the store and its property until it's torn down. You were there when whatever happened happened." I paused for effect. "So, what happened?"

"No idea," he said. His voice was matter-of-fact and sounded as if he were beginning to wonder about my sanity.

I was beginning to wonder about it too.

"How can you *not* know? You were there, weren't you?"

"I suppose."

"Since you can't leave without my permission, I'd say that's a big yes," I said. "And elves don't sleep, do they?"

"Thankfully."

"So, what happened to our dead guy? How did he get inside the store?" I knew better than to ask him who the dead guy was. After all, to Peppermint, all humans looked alike. "Who killed him?" I took a breath. My voice was rising, and I needed to calm down.

"I don't know. I didn't see what happened."

I blinked at the steering wheel, uncertain where the mischievous little pain in my rear was sitting. My only hope was that if my stare could shoot lasers, I'd get lucky and accidentally get him.

"I'm serious, Thomas," Peppermint said. "This is troubling for me as well. Last thing I remember was Trixie locking up the shop last night, then you calling my name and summoning me here. I'm not messing with you."

I took a step back at that. Elves have perfect memories. They don't forget. Oddly, despite the incorporeal form, they have been known to get intoxicated from honey-based liquors like mead and lose track of time. Then again, time has very little meaning for their kind.

"Were you drinking last night?" I asked him.

Silence.

"If you're shaking your head or nodding, remember...I can't see you in this sunlight."

There was still silence.

"Peppermint." My voice dripped with ire. Despite his animosity toward me, I was still his master, and he knew it.

"All right. Perhaps I ducked into your stash of Yuletide mead after you left the store yesterday."

I shook my head, trying hard not to roll my eyes. You might be wondering how a spirit being like an elf can consume anything material, especially alcohol. I'm still trying to wrap my head around that concept too. But I know they can turn freshly churned milk into a kind of alcoholic smoothie, and they enjoy tobacco and candy too. And somehow these physical substances can have peculiar effects on their incorporeal forms.

Hey, it's folklore, not science. I don't know everything about this stuff. Just more than most.

Then, something he'd said a few minutes ago came back to me. "You saw Trixie closing up Wonderland yesterday?"

"Yes, I did. She told me she was heading over to that scoundrel Seth Timmons's house to study for her psych exam." He mumbled something under his breath, then added, "We really should do something about that malcontent. I don't like him one bit."

I agreed with the elf in that vein, but dwelling on it wasn't going to solve our issue right now.

Or maybe it will.

I stood up to my full height as an idea struck me. I reached for my phone and scrolled through my contacts until I came to Seth's number, then pressed the call button. Three rings later, someone picked up.

"Dude, it's early," Seth Timmons's surfer-boy voice echoed back at me. "Why are you calling this early, Mr. Nast?"

"Seth, have you seen Trixie?" I asked.

"Trixie, er..." The kid seemed like he was still half asleep. He sniffed into the phone, then I heard a rustle of noise as if he were shifting in his bed. "Not since last night," he finally said. "We went out after studying. Had a few drinks." He paused again. "Actually, she had quite a few. Shots of whiskey. She was pretty hammered, but..."

"Seth, focus. When did you last see her?"

"Mmmm...around midnight, I guess. A couple of hours before Stuart's closed."

Stuart's Pub. Just a couple of blocks from here.

"Did she drive home, or did you take her?"

I was getting really worried now. Trix could put down some booze when she wanted to. It was one of the last remaining vestiges of her old rebellious lifestyle.

"Um, neither. She decided to stay a while longer. Said she'd either take an Uber home or just walk to your store and sleep it off. That's why—"

I'd already hung up the phone and was running toward Wonderland's porch when one of the uniformed deputies stopped me in my tracks.

"Sorry, sir, you can't go in there."

"I need to get in there. I think Trixie McNamara, my employee, might be inside. She might be hurt!"

Or worse. I shuddered at the thought.

The deputy shook his head. "We searched the whole place," he said, patting my shoulder in an attempt to calm me. "No one else is inside."

I took a step back and glanced up at the old Victorian house that now contained Wonderland within its ancient walls. The place was immense. Three stories, if you counted the fully furnished apartment space in the turret, and it was littered with a honeycomb of secret passages and hidden nooks that Horatio Longpepper had added over the years to build the store's sense of mystery and wonder. As strange as it sounds, the House itself had added a few secrets of its own, including a thirteen-foot guard-alligator we called Tinsel inhabiting its walls. There were literally dozens of places Trixie could be hidden without anyone but myself and Peppermint being able to find her—at least without getting hopelessly lost, hurt by some odd booby trap, or eaten by the gator. The place was dangerous for the uninitiated or uninvited.

"You don't understand," I said. "There are places inside the shop you'd never know to look. I need to—"

"What's going on out here?" It was a woman's voice coming from the front door. The female detective.

I brushed past the deputy. "Detective Lassiter, I've got to get inside. My employee, Trixie, hasn't shown up to work yet. It's not like her, and I think she might be somewhere inside the store."

Lassiter eyed me up and down, an air of suspicion etched on her cold, but rather lovely, face.

"Just a sec," she said before returning inside.

I stood at the foot of the porch steps, waiting. The deputy who had stopped me from rushing into the shop kept a careful watch on me, but had given me some space.

"Pep," I whispered.

"Already on it," he replied as a gentle scent hinting of licorice and honeysuckle swept past me.

If I couldn't get inside, then at least Peppermint could search high and low for her without the police ever being the wiser.

Then there was the House itself. It wasn't exactly your average turn-of-the-century building and didn't take kindly to strangers exploring its secrets. It could tolerate the customers and gawkers who stayed on the first two floors and the designated shopping areas, but it was none too keen on anyone going anywhere it didn't want them to. The passages and nooks were just such places.

A minute later, Detective Lassiter came back out and took the two steps necessary to meet me. "I'm sorry, sir. Until Crime Scene has a chance to photograph and process everything, no one can go inside." She glanced over at the uniformed deputy behind me. "But our guys searched the place high and low. No one was inside."

I explained to her about the conversation I'd just had with Seth Timmons, and his revelation that Trixie had planned to sleep off a bender at the shop earlier this morning. I then told her about the secret passages and hiding places scattered throughout the old place. She asked me for details about the passages, but I wasn't a fan of that line of questioning one bit. The passages that Horatio had constructed were relatively safe, but the House wasn't going to like the police poking around those it had chosen to add on its own. Besides that, there was one room in the shop that I, personally, didn't want anyone to find. One room, in fact, that no one could ever enter but me.

I was pretty sure they'd never be able to locate it, even with a detailed run-down of the passages—the House would take care of that—but I didn't know if I could afford to take the chance.

But Trixie's life might be in danger.

That single thought brought everything into crystal clarity. I asked the detective to hold on for a minute. Then, digging in my suit pockets, I pulled out a notepad and several colored pens and diagramed as much of the House's interior as I could remember. Given that the passages were prone to change frequently on the House's whims, I couldn't be sure the map would be any help at all. But it was all I could do. After a minute or two, I handed the crudely scrawled map to the detective.

"Green lines show safe, easy passages to follow," I told her. "Red lines...well, let's just say they can get a little wonky if you're not careful."

"'Wonky'?"

"Tricky to navigate," I said. "Easy to get turned around in. That's all."

That was a bald-faced lie—it was so much more than that—and I hoped I wouldn't regret it later.

As the detective took the map of the house from me, she gave me a nod of thanks and went back inside. When she disappeared, I turned to the shop's front door and whispered, "Pep, tell the House to let them search. Don't give them a hard time."

I wasn't sure whether the elf heard me or if the House would listen, so I paced back and forth for more than an hour, waiting for news from either Lassiter or Pep. The sun's rays burned down on my shoulders, making me uncomfortably warm in my pinstriped suit. I slipped out of the jacket and placed it carefully on the front seat of my car before straightening both my tie and my waistcoat.

Come on, Trix. Where are you?

Cars drove back and forth along Comet Avenue, their passengers' heads turning toward my shop, no doubt curious as to what had drawn the police. I wanted to yell at them. Tell them to keep driving and mind their own business. That a man was dead, and they should show a little respect. But I knew it wouldn't do any good. People were ghouls when it came to this kind of thing. It was in their nature. Especially here in Christmas, where nothing exciting ever really happens.

I let out a frustrated breath, wondering what was taking so long.

"Tom, we've got trouble," Peppermint suddenly said from my back seat.

When I jumped from surprise, the deputy near the house turned and cocked his head at me. I pretended to stretch my arms while waving back at him with a shrug. Hopefully, he'd think I was simply on edge. But not *suspiciously* on edge.

"What? Was Trixie inside? Is she okay?"

"Oh, she was inside. Besides being passed out with a hum-dinger of a hangover, she is *physically* okay, yes."

"Then what's the prob—"

My question caught in my throat as the front door opened, and Trixie McNamara was led out of my store in handcuffs. She was dressed all in black, normal for her, considering that she was what the kids today referred to as a Goth. A black choker collar and a myriad of silver necklaces with an assortment of crucifixes hung down from her slender neck. Her jet-black hair, streaked here and there with flashes of green, hung over her face as she was led down the steps.

"What's going on?" I shouted, racing over to detectives Tice and Lassiter. As I approached, Trixie looked up at me, and I could finally make out her face through her tussle of hair. Her burgundy lipstick looked the same as when I'd last seen her yes-terday, but her cheeks were smeared nearly black from where her mascara had run from drying tears. But that wasn't the only thing I noticed as I drew closer. Her arms and neck were covered in something red—dark red—and I nearly gasped at the sight.

"Is...is that blood?" I asked, looking at the detectives.

Tice, holding his hands out to me in a warning to stay back, shook his head. "No, sir. We found her lying on a bed of holly in one of those passages you told us about. Some of the berries were crushed when we tried to apprehend her, and the juice got all over her."

"Apprehend her? Why did you need to apprehend her? She had every right to be in the store. She hadn't broken in. She's the store's manag—"

Tice interrupted my protests. "Mr. Nast, I'm sorry to inform you, but we have very good reason to believe she is responsible for the death of Mr. Hank Cobb."

"We're taking her to the Sheriff's Office to question her further," Lassiter continued.

Hank Cobb? He was the sixth person I'd given the pocket-knife to. The one who had fallen on such hard times.

"Oh, dear Lord." It felt as though my world had just dropped out of the sky. My knees threatened to buckle under me from the news. "That's...that's Hank Cobb in there?" I pointed to Wonderland.

"We believe so, yes. ID we found in his pocket matched his face when we removed the beard."

I looked at Trixie, who was unusually quiet, and saw the tears returning from the corners of her eyes like a busted dam. It didn't take much to understand why. Not only was she being accused of murder, but the murder of Henry Cobb, Jr.—her biological and horribly abusive father.

"Trix?" I stooped down to look her in the face. At over six-foot-eight, I had to do that with most people anyway. Even more so, now that she refused to look me in the eye. "What happened last night?"

She glanced up at me and gave me an imperceptible shake of her head. She wasn't sure. Like Pep, she had no recollection of the night before.

I turned my attention to the detectives. "What makes you think she has anything to do with his death?"

Tice pulled me aside as his partner continued walking Trixie to their detective car.

"Don't worry, Trixie!" I shouted at her as she was led away. "I'll call Ursula!" Then I turned my attention back to Tice. "Okay. So why do you think she killed him, exactly?"

He didn't answer me right away. Instead, he reached into a pocket and pulled out a plastic evidence bag. He unfurled the bag and held it up to me. "Have you ever seen this knife before?"

The bag contained the blood-soaked Swiss Army Knife I'd seen earlier.

I could only nod in response.

"Thought you might." He nodded at the emblem embedded on the handle. "The Christmas tree kind of gave it away."

"I gave it, along with five others, to several of my friends over a decade ago," I said. "Hank was one of them."

Tice's eyes widened. "You were friends? With Hank Cobb? The way I hear it, the guy is a real piece of work. A rap sheet a mile long, including burglary, drug possession, DUI, fraud, battery, and much, much more." He paused. I had the feeling it was for effect. "Not to mention child abuse and endangerment to a... one Tricia Ella McNamara."

I sighed. "We were friends a long time ago, yeah," I responded. "Good ones. He played Santa for the YMCA in Winter Haven every year. Had a decent job. A pillar of the community. Then, about twelve years ago, his wife left him and Trixie for another man. Hank blamed Trix. Turned to the bottle. And everything went downhill from there."

Tice nodded as if he understood. In his line of work, he probably did. Probably saw similar stories every day.

I pointed at the knife. "Is that his?" I asked. "Hank's, I mean."

The detective held it up for a better look, then shrugged. "Any way to know for sure? Initials or anything?"

I shook my head. "All six were identical."

"Then no, we haven't verified that it belongs to him. We'll need a list of the other five who received one of your knives, though." He handed me a business card. "Do me a favor and just email me a list, with contact information, as soon as you can."

I nodded. "But I still don't understand why you automatically assume Trixie is the kill—"

"Not killer," he interrupted me. "Not even a suspect yet. Think of her as a person of interest at this point."

"But why? Other than the fact that they are related and that she was sleeping a bender off in the store, why is she even a person of interest?"

"Because of a 911 call we got last night," he explained. "A report of a pretty nasty argument between a man dressed in a Santa suit and a woman matching Ms. McNamara's description. By the time our patrol guys arrived, both were gone, but a witness claimed the man—who we believe to be Hank Cobb—had struck her. Knocked her down, then took off. The girl reportedly started chasing him, and that was the last time either of them was seen until today."

I shook my head. "She didn't do it," I said, wishing I sounded more convincing. The truth was that Trixie and her father had never gotten along. He'd been a decent fellow once upon a time. Happy. Easy with a laugh. Even easier to rely on. He was one of the best Santas I knew, and that's saying something.

Then, Trixie's mom had left him for her boss. They took off to God knows where, leaving both Hank and Trix alone to fend for themselves. Hank couldn't cope. He turned to the bottle and became a mean drunk. The meaner he got, the more morose. He hated his wife. Hated himself even more. But he took it all out on the nine-year-old Trixie, blaming her for everything. Eventually, unable to take the abuse anymore, she ran away and did whatever she needed to do to survive. Burglary, shoplifting, even drugs. When I'd caught her stealing from the store and offered her a deal to work for me instead of going to jail, she had been a girl full of venom and loathing. Most of that loathing had been focused on herself, but there was a good portion directed toward her father. But in the three and a half years that she'd worked for me—had become my protégé—she'd changed. She was happy. Was working on her bachelor's degree in business to turn her life around. She hoped to take over the shop one day, even. I just couldn't see her ruining all that over a drunken brawl with her dad.

Detective Tice gave me a doubtful look.

"I'm telling you: she didn't do it."

"Forgive me if I don't take your word for it." He started making his way to his car, then stopped. "I still have more questions for you, Mr. Nast. I hope you'll make yourself available in the coming days."

Translation: "Don't leave town."

"And don't forget to email me that list of recipients of those special little knives of yours, okay?" He cast me a wink and clicked his tongue before climbing into the passenger side of the unmarked car.

I bit down on my lip. While I couldn't necessarily say there was something about the detective to dislike, he did rub me the wrong way, and it wasn't completely because he was arresting a girl I'd come to think of as a daughter over the years.

"Trust me, Detective," I said to no one, as his partner drove him out of the parking lot. "You'll be seeing a whole lot of me until this mess is taken care of."

3

It was another five and a half hours or so before Crime Scene finished processing everything and the body was wheeled out by the Medical Examiner's removal team. As the road deputies pulled away, I was given the all-clear to reenter my store and get back to my daily business. Once inside, I emailed the list of names that had received my Christmas knives to Detective Tice, then gave George Trabor a quick call to let him know I wasn't going to open the shop today. I ended up promising to deliver what he needed later that afternoon.

After that, I stood at the counter next to my register and blew out another irritated breath.

"Oh, Trixie, what have you gotten yourself into this time?" I mumbled.

I knew what must be done, but I was loath to do it. Though it had been one of the most difficult things I'd ever had to do, I had spent the better part of a year trying to break free of Ursula Brooks and her amorous affections toward me; and now that she had pretty much stopped calling me every other day, I was going to have to break the reprieve I'd worked so hard to build.

I picked up the phone and punched in the number I knew by heart.

"Tate, Higgins, and Smith," came a soft feminine voice on the other end. "This line is recorded for quality-assurance purposes."

"Hey, Janet," I said into the phone. "This is Tom. Tom Nast. Is Ursula around?"

"Oh, Mr...eh...Nast." Janet Wood, the law firm's paralegal and administrative assistant, sounded more flustered than usual. "How are you, er, doing? It's been a while."

Janet and my ex-girlfriend Ursula were best friends. Thick as thieves. She'd never liked me much. From the moment of our breakup, she'd been both overjoyed that I was finally out of the picture and overly protective of Ursula's feelings. I figured she was none too happy to hear from me right now. It was also probably killing her that she was required to be polite to me over the firm's telephone—which, as she had reminded me when she answered, is always recorded.

"Yes, it has." I cleared my throat. "Is everything okay, Janet? If this is a bad time, I can..."

"No!" She paused, as if realizing she'd just said the word far too loudly. I rolled my eyes. The woman had always been overly dramatic. A diva if there ever was one. But she was really putting it on thick right now. "Just a second, Tom. I think she's just finishing up with a client."

I heard a click, and the easy-listening sound of hold Muzak filled my ear.

"So, you're going to bring that train wreck back into our lives again, then?" I turned to see the faintest hint of a diminutive human outline standing in front of the red and green lights of the store's primary Christmas tree. The lighting still wasn't optimal for seeing my elfin servant fully, but it was close.

"Come on," I said. "She's a great person. I thought she was The One until..."

"Until she found out who you really were and tore out your heart before stomping on it?"

It wasn't exactly how our relationship had ended, but Peppermint enjoyed being just as dramatic as Janet when the mood struck him. In fact, I was the one who had ended things with Ursula; and, to this day, she had no idea why. He was partially right, but it had been me who had told her my secret. Yes, she couldn't handle it. And yes, it did break my heart. Not that she can remember any of it, mind you. That part of our breakup, unfortunately, had been stricken from her memory.

"Believe me," I said. "I'm not any happier about having to call her than you are."

"Then hang up the phone."

I shrugged. "Can't. Trixie needs legal help; and no matter how things ended between Ursula and me, she's one of the best lawyers around."

"So you think our girl is guilty?"

"No, of course not." A lump swelled in my throat, a symptom that happens every time I lie about something. Or, in this case, when I wasn't a hundred percent sure. "But better to be prepared and line up a good defense attorney in advance."

I heard the elf grunt; then he disappeared from view.

Ignoring the elf-equivalent of a temper tantrum, I started drumming my fingers on the countertop while listening to the hold music. As I did, my eyes scanned my showroom floor. It was impressive, even by *my* standards, with a domed ceiling twenty-six feet high painted like a winter wonderland and twinkling white Christmas lights strung from rafter to rafter. Although most of the floor was hand-hewn marble imported from Egypt, the atrium, which was where the large primary Christmas tree sat—and, until recently, a dead body—was covered in mahogany hardwood flooring. Seven marble pillars held up a section of the second floor, which overlooked the first. Everywhere you looked, toy planes, model trains, mechanical robots, and all manner of other toys hummed, warbled, and zoomed.

I glanced over to the tree and at the area where I'd discovered Hank Cobb's body, and I tried to visualize him still lying there.

Hank had always been a big guy. Not only broad in chest and shoulder, but tall too. Almost as tall as me. But I have more of a Jack Skellington, Ichabod Crane, scarecrow build. Hank was more of a grizzly bear. That should have been the big clue for me when I first saw him this morning. None of my other customers were nearly as tall. But then, Hank wasn't exactly a customer anymore. And nowhere I could think of would even consider letting him play Santa for kids. I hadn't suspected him of being the corpse simply because he and Santa cosplaying were a ridiculous juxtaposition I couldn't even comprehend.

Which begged the question: why *was* Hank dressed as Santa? What was he up to?

My eyes drifted up to the domed ceiling over where his body had lain. There was an eighteen-inch ball of mistletoe, tied in bright red ribbons, hanging from the overhead rafters that connected portions of the second-floor landing to the pillars.

"Tom?" A voice on the other end of the phone interrupted my train of thought.

Caught off guard, I fumbled the receiver, nearly dropping it, then brought it to my ear.

"Ursula? Is that you?"

There was a pause. "Wow. I honestly never thought I'd be hearing from you again."

If she could have seen me through the phone, she would have seen my face turn sugar-plum red. I'll admit it: I'd been a real jerk to the woman; but I had felt it the best way to handle the breakup, given the circumstances.

"Hey, Ursula, I know. Yeah. I'm sorry about all—"

"What can I do for you, Tom?" She cut me off. All business. I couldn't decide whether that was a good or a bad thing.

She's a woman, Tom. It's never a good thing.

"It's Trix, actually," I said. "She needs your help."

That seemed to rein in Ursula's contempt for me. "What happened?"

I explained the events of the morning, describing the body and his relationship with Trixie. Then I told her how the detectives had led her out of Wonderland in handcuffs, claiming they were simply taking her to the station to question her.

"Oh, heck no," she practically growled into the phone. "Not my little Trixie. I'll be in touch."

And with that she hung up the phone. Ursula's immediate action didn't surprise me. Trixie was special to quite a few people in our community. Everyone loved her—at least anyone who made the effort to get past her dark Goth exterior, anyway. Most people in Christmas would bend over backward to take care of her in a time of need. Ursula was no different. In fact, she and Trixie had developed quite a special bond during the time she and I had dated. I had no trouble picturing the tough-as-nails attorney storming out of her office, jumping into her late-model Audi, and hightailing it to the Sheriff's Office as counsel for the defense.

I kind of felt sorry for Tice and Lassiter. But only kind of.

"So it's done, then," Peppermint said. I couldn't quite tell where he was when he said it. His voice seemed to echo from all directions. "Unleashed the crazed beast, have we?"

Rolling my eyes, I ignored his jab. "I need you to do something," I told him.

"O, great master," he replied. "I live to serve. Your wish is my command. Open sesame."

I stifled a groan at his sarcasm. "Talk to the House. See what it can tell you about what happened last night."

There was a flash of movement to my left, and I turned to see the fully formed figure of the elf underneath the massive Christmas tree.

If you're wondering what an elf looks like when they do allow you to see them, look at yourself in a fun-house mirror and you'll get a pretty good idea. They're mimics. Chameleons. They naturally appear as smaller, out-of-proportion replicas of the person seeing them. Only their faces appear more childlike. Softer, with no hard lines. Their noses are barely noticeable and their cheeks are exaggerated, the only portion of their bodies that isn't porcelain white—in fact, they're often red. Their eyes are bigger, brighter, with large black pupils. They are completely hairless except for a little bit of fuzz where their eyebrows should be. And yes, they do have pointy ears.

At that moment, Pep's orange-red eyebrows—mirrors of my own hair color—were arched as if he thought I was the biggest idiot on the planet.

"You know it doesn't work like that, Master Thomas." Whenever Peppermint got especially irked with me, he overemphasized the master/servant nature of our relationship. "The House doesn't speak. Not even to me. I can get sensations from it, naturally. But it doesn't communicate with words or even ideas. Not like us." He shrugged. "Or, rather, like me. I'm not entirely sure you communicate with words or ideas either. At least, not intelligent ones."

"Please. Just give it a try. For Trixie's sake."

He disappeared, and I walked over to the spot where Hank Cobb had been found. There wasn't a whole lot to see. There had been a good bit of blood that had pooled around the body overnight, but it was already dissolving before my eyes. The House could never tolerate a mess, after all, and it was already hard at work cleaning up what remained of the dead man. When I reflected on it, I realized we were probably quite lucky that it hadn't simply swallowed the entire corpse before I came home this morning. Then again, that might have been a blessing.

Getting down on my hands and knees, I pressed my face against the floor a few inches from the spots of blood that remained and searched for clues. To my right, there was nothing but floor space, the base of one of our smaller Christmas trees with silver-colored branches and bright red balls. There were a few carved-wood toys around the tree, and just past them was a door that led to the customer bathroom. To my left, a few feet away, sat an antique claw-footed settee. I peered underneath it, and something caught my eye. I moved over to the couch, lay down on the floor, and reached out for the object. When I withdrew my hand, I found that I was holding a coin of some kind.

Examining it closely, I realized it wasn't a coin at all, but rather a token. An *Alcoholics Anonymous* six-month sobriety chip. I flipped it over for closer inspection, but there was nothing about it to tell me where it might have come from or who might have dropped it. For all I knew, it had been dropped some time ago by a customer and had been long forgotten. Then again, knowing the House's propensity to tidy up even the most minuscule of debris, chances were good that it might have been dropped by the killer—since I highly doubted Hank Cobb had ever bothered to go to an AA meeting in his life.

Pocketing the token in my coat, I climbed to my feet and scanned the room one more time with nothing to show for it. Either the cops had done a thorough job collecting whatever evidence had remained, the killer had left no other clues, or my sentient and severely compulsive domicile had already tidied everything up that might have been useful.

I started lowering myself to sit down and think about everything and, like clockwork, my favorite reading chair whipped across the floor to catch my bottom just as I dropped. A moment later, an antique end table with a cup of steaming hot tea slid into place next to me. I picked the porcelain cup up and drank from it.

By now, you're probably thinking there's something mighty strange about this Thomas Nast and his *Wonderland Christmas and Holiday Emporium*, and you'd be right in that assumption. I'm going to let you in on a little secret, known to only a handful of people on Earth—Trixie and Peppermint included.

See, my dad died in a plane crash when I was still in diapers. My mother, they say, died of a broken heart a few years later. After that, I stayed with my aunt for a brief time, but she wasn't exactly keen on children. So she gave me up after about a year, and I entered the foster-care system. I won't go into details about all that—it's a story for another time—but needless to say, I eventually made the acquaintance of Krin'Ghal, better known to Americans as Kris Kringle. St. Nick. Or Santa Claus, if you prefer.

Yes, he's real. Though, like the elves of mythology, he's not exactly what the average person believes him to be. Like the elves, he's more spirit than physical specimen, although he does inhabit the body of a willing human to carry out his Yuletide deeds. The current person to house old St. Nick is now two hundred and thirty-three years old, but he's not long for this world. When his time is up, it was initially going to be Horatio Longpepper picking up the mantle. But with Horatio now gone, the mantle has fallen to me. This is a rather tricky proposition for me, because A) I don't like the cold—hello? North Pole?—and B) I take after my aunt in regard to children. I find them to be generally sticky. And smelly. So, not a big fan, although I've been assured that when the time comes, so will my love for kids.

I'll believe that when I see it, but Christmas is all about faith. And I've put my faith exactly where it needs to be: with the One who brought the spirit of Christmas into the world to begin with. I figure He knows what He's doing.

I'm telling you all this so that you'll have a better understanding of all the magic surrounding my life, as well as to explain how frustrated I currently was over feeling so powerless to help Trixie in her current legal crisis. After all, as the song says, "He knows when you've been bad or good," so I was pretty much asking myself how I couldn't know who'd committed murder in my own little sanctuary.

It was bad enough that a person's life had been taken; but to do it here, of all places. There was something almost blasphemous about it to me.

I took another sip of tea, careful not to allow it to burn my tongue, and considered everything I knew so far about the murder. There wasn't much. Hank Cobb had been killed. Presumably from multiple stab wounds. And more than likely with one of the six knives I'd given away as gifts to some of my closest friends.

I pondered that last morsel a few minutes. The very thought of it tasted like ash in my mouth. My friends. I could imagine none of them as murderers. Hank Cobb had been a recipient of one of the knives and, even as bad as he turned out, I couldn't begin to imagine him as a killer. It just seemed so preposterous. These were good men with generous hearts. Christmas was everything to them. Children and their innocence are what drove most of them in life. The whole aspect of murder would be anathema to them.

I sat there for a few more minutes, staring off into space.

"Like I said..." Peppermint's voice startled me. I spun my head, looking for the source, but once again the elf was invisible. "...the House was mum about the killing."

I shook my head, not really surprised, and sank back in my chair.

"So, Sherlock," Pep continued, "I take it from that glum expression on your freckled face that you're planning on trying to solve this murder yourself?"

I threw him an irritated scowl. My brow furrowed as I considered his question. I'd honestly not even toyed with the idea. I'd simply been trying to understand the course of events that had turned my day, as well as my gut, into an enormous pretzel. But the more I thought about it, the more I knew Pep was probably right. The more I dwelt on the fact that a life had been taken within these hallowed walls, the angrier I became. And the pinnacle of it all was the fact that Trixie, in almost all respects my surrogate daughter, was all but being accused of murdering her real father. Knowing the Orange County Sheriff's Office the way I did, one look at her rap sheet and they'd pretty much figure they had their culprit. Whether they really believed she was simply a "person of interest" or not, they wouldn't look too hard anywhere else.

No, if I couldn't figure out what had happened here last night and clear Trix's name, then I had no business ever considering myself worthy of the mantel of Krin'Ghal.

I offered the invisible elf a wry smile, then nodded. "Yeah," I said, standing from the reading chair and grabbing my coat off the counter. "I guess I am."

4

'd never been to Stuart's Pub. Honestly, never been to any pubs really. Doesn't exactly go with the whole "Santa" vibe. But considering that it was the last place anyone had seen Hank Cobb alive, I figured it was as good a place as any to start my little investigation.

I left Wonderland and drove the quarter of a mile east to the seedy dive bar on the edge of town. It was just past noon, and the parking lot was already full of beat-up old pickup trucks, motor-cycles, and at least one bicycle chained to the pub's street sign.

The thought of Trixie frequenting this place sent a wave of sadness through me. She'd come so far in such a short amount of time, but the girl still liked to party a little too hard. Something I figured she'd inherited from her father. And Stuart's was the only bar in town, unless you wanted to drive into the insane traf-fic of Interstate 4 to Orlando.

Putting the Thunderbird in park, I climbed out of the driv-er's seat, straightened my tie, and grabbed my cane from the front seat. The cane wasn't necessary, of course. I had no trouble am-bulating. But given that I was wearing a green suit with red pin-stripes, a bright red tie, and a hunter-green derby hat, I figured the cane completed the ensemble. Plus, this particular cane—with its rather unusual properties—could come in handy in a pinch. And considering the bar's particular clientele, you never knew when you might need something special to pull you out of a mess. I can't say I was going to blend in very well at Stuart's, but at that moment, I really didn't care. I had a job to do.

The moment I stepped inside, every eye turned to me, and my already-ruddy cheeks turned the color of my ginger hair. I swallowed, glanced around the room, and strode over to the bar where a surly bartender, whose arms were covered in some rather lewd tattoos, narrowed his eyes at me.

"What can I get for you?" he asked, wiping away grime from a glass with a surprisingly clean washcloth.

I smiled at him, hoping to ease the tension. But I realized the only one feeling tension in this situation was me.

"Information," I said, climbing up onto a stool next to a biker who was snoring so loudly he nearly drowned out the jukebox playing in the background.

The bartender, who I assumed was Stuart himself, laughed. "Sorry. We don't serve that here."

Afraid we'd gotten off on the wrong foot, I changed tactics. "I'm not a police officer."

This time, his laugh was louder than the snoring biker. "No, duh. Ain't seen too many cops dressed like a candy cane before." He set the now-clean glass down and started working on another. "Still, we serve drinks. Some music. Maybe even a few laughs. But information ain't something we keep in stock around here. So, either order a drink, put a quarter in the box, or *sayonara.*"

On a hunch, I tried yet another tack, hoping the third time truly would be the charm.

"It's about Hank Cobb."

Stuart stopped polishing the glass. One eyebrow perked up. "Oh, really? What's that clown done now?"

"Died," I said flatly.

One of the bartender's eyebrows arched. "Really?" He shook

his head in disbelief. "Wow. I just saw him last night. Seemed perfectly healthy to me. What happened?"

I sighed, then nodded over to the soda fountain on the other side of the bar. "Can I have a root beer, please?"

He poured a mug and handed it to me. After I took a swig, I looked up at him. "He was murdered sometime last night. Looks like he was stabbed in the back." I went on to explain the morning I'd been having and the fact that I'd heard that the last place he'd been seen was at the bar. "So I'm kind of hoping to find out everything I can about him and who might want him dead."

"Well, for Trixie's sake, I think I can make an exception." Stuart blew out a breath and set the glass he was cleaning down on the counter before peering through the crowded room. A moment later, a look of recognition dawned on his face, and he nodded across the room to a booth toward the back. "See that fella over there?"

I turned to look and found a small, elderly Hispanic-looking man with a John Deere cap staring down into a half-empty mug of beer. He wore mechanic's coveralls with a name patch over his left breast pocket that read "Jose."

"That's Jose Jimenez. He's the guy who saw Hank fighting with Trixie last night," he said. "I reckon he can tell you all about it."

I nodded my thanks, but before I left, a question sprang to mind. "Did Hank have any enemies?"

Stuart guffawed. "Better question is whether he had any friends. Dude was not well liked around here, mostly 'cause he mooched off other customers, begging for booze. But he'd also swindled a few of my regulars out of some money."

"And are these the kind of people who might have no problem stabbing a man in the back?"

His eyes narrowed, as if struggling with how much he should say. "These dudes ain't exactly church-going folks, if that's what you mean."

"Any chance you can give me some names?"

"I dunno. Any chance I won't kick you out of my place for asking too many dumb questions?"

Taking his meaning loud and clear, I paid him for the soda and headed over to the booth where Jose still pondered the mysteries of his beer mug. As I approached, the spell he was in seemed to break, and he looked up at me.

"Hi, there." I waved, then pointed to the seat across from him. "Mind if I sit down for a second?"

He glanced around, as if trying to figure out where Allen Funt might be hiding, then shrugged. "Free country."

Taking the seat, I stared across the booth at him, but he'd already returned his gaze to the amber-foam-topped liquid in his glass. To me, it seemed like he had something heavy on his mind, but it could just as easily have been alcohol clouding it as anything else.

"So, I understand you saw Hank Cobb last night, fighting with a girl in the parking lot?" I decided cutting to the chase would be best for both of us. I had a feeling this guy wasn't going to be very patient with me. Besides, since I had no real clue on how to conduct a murder investigation, I was taking my cue from the slew of cop shows I've watched my whole life.

He looked up at me, and his brows furrowed. "You a cop?"

"Do I look like a cop?" I smiled. "Actually, name's Thomas Nast. I own the Wonderland Christmas and Holiday Emporium a few blocks away."

The guy seemed to ponder that for a moment, then his eyes brightened. "Oh, yeah! I know that place." Besides his words being slightly slurred, he had a heavy Latin accent. "*Pai Natal* and all that."

Pai Natal was the Portuguese term for Santa Claus, which made him more than likely Brazilian.

"Exactly." I took another sip of my root beer. "Look, the girl you saw fighting with Hank was his daughter. She's being accused of killing him, and I'm trying to prove she didn't do it. Anything you can tell me might help."

"Señor Cobb is dead?"

"Yes. Murdered in my shop last night."

Jose stared at me a moment, then shrugged. "Bummer."

"You could say that. Especially considering a very good friend of mine—not to mention Cobb's own daughter—is the lead suspect. So I need to know: What happened last night?"

"Everything I saw, I told the police."

"Yes, but, like I said, I'm not *with* the police."

He lifted his beer glass and downed the remaining contents before wiping his mouth with his shirt sleeve.

"Look, I don't want no trouble," he said. "I wouldn't have called the cops if that girl hadn't been screaming her head off at Hank. I thought she was going to kill him then and there. You ask me, the police got the right person."

That wasn't good news at all. If he'd told the cops that, no wonder they were looking at Trixie for the murder.

"Please," I said, leaning forward and forcing him to look me in the eye. "I know this girl. I know she couldn't have done it. I have to find out the truth."

"Señor...what was your name again?"

"Nast. Tom Nast."

"Señor Nast, understand. The girl was very angry. She said things to Hank last night. Vile things. Threats." He paused, considering his words. "Hank Cobb has that effect on people. There's more than a handful in this bar right now who've made similar threats to that drunk on more than one occasion. But the look in her eyes last night told me everything. She wanted him dead. For real."

"So, tell me. What were they arguing about?"

"I...I don't know," he said. "Just caught the tail end of the fight. But it got physical. Hank pushed her to the ground, and she got up swinging."

I could see Trix doing that. She still wasn't as ladylike as I want to believe. Still has some of that juvenile-delinquent fire in her. But I didn't want to focus on her. Right now, I wanted to stay on Hank Cobb. Although I'd seen him around once or twice over the years since his plunge into the bottle, I didn't know very much about the man he had become. And Trixie rarely ever spoke of him. What I *did* know came from snippets I'd heard here and there from other residents of Christmas.

I took another swig from my mug and, once again, tried to steer the conversation in another direction. "Did you know Hank well?"

Jose shrugged. "About as well as anyone here did, I guess."

I looked at the man's mechanic's overalls. Hank had never maintained any steady employment since his wife left him. From what I understood, he'd become a bit of a rogue. As the bartender had confirmed, he'd been a con man to some. A hustler. He'd done odd jobs here and there for a variety of unsavory types. But besides drinking alcohol, his one real passion in life that had never disappeared had been cars—especially classic ones. He'd found my Thunderbird, told me about it, and then souped it up after I'd purchased it. In recent years, I'd caught him eyeing it on more than one occasion, and part of me was concerned that he was thinking of stealing it. But, just like anything in Wonderland, it wouldn't have gone very well for him if he'd tried.

"Did Hank ever work for you, Jose?" I nodded to the stitched name tag on his coveralls. "I know how much he loved cars."

He nodded. "We were business partners from time to time, but it rarely ever paid off."

I could only imagine what sort of business these two were in together.

"Could any of those business ventures possibly lead to someone killing him?"

The Brazilian eyed me warily. His mouth clenched tight, and I could see him grinding away at his teeth. I think I'd struck a nerve.

"You sure you ain't a cop?"

"Trust me." I smiled back at him. "I'm about as much a cop as I am Santa Claus."

The instant the words were out of my mouth, I regretted it. There was a loud scratch as the jukebox near us suddenly stopped playing Hank Williams and was instantly replaced by Burl Ives singing "A Holly Jolly Christmas." I closed my eyes, pinching the bridge of my nose in irritation.

"Hey!" Stuart the bartender shouted at no one in particular. "Who the heck picked this garbage? I didn't even know that song was in the box!"

Yeah, this kind of thing happens to me from time to time. Any mention of Krin'Ghal or Christmas can set off some rather weird Yuletide miracles around me. There was a good chance Stuart was right and the jukebox didn't even have the song in its repertoire.

When I looked over at Jose, he was staring back down into his now-empty mug. "I think you should leave," he said. "I'm done talking. Just want to drink in peace."

It couldn't end this way. I had too many questions that needed answers. Then a thought struck me.

"Why aren't you at work today, Jose?" I pulled a fob watch from my vest and pointed down at the time. "It's the middle of the day. Why aren't you working?"

The more I thought about it, the more I found it odd that Jose hadn't sounded the least upset over the news that his occasional business partner was dead. *Bummer*, he'd said. Not very broken up about it. Definitely not surprised. It was almost as if he'd known already. Christmas is small, but not small enough for news of Hank's death to have traveled to Stuart's Pub yet. The bartender himself was proof of that.

Jose looked at me. "I don't see how that's any of your business."

Burl Ives was still belting out his Christmas jingle in the background and should have set me in a festive mood. Instead, the way Jose's eyes glared at me over the rim of his mug caused a lump to swell in my throat.

"Just...just curious," I said. "Thought it was odd that a car mechanic would take the day off during the week."

Most mechanics I know, if they're even remotely good—or honest—pretty much stay busy twenty-four/seven. They rarely ever close, except for maybe Sundays and very special holidays.

"I think I'd like to drink alone now, *por favor.*"

He might have said please, but from the tone of his voice it didn't sound like a request.

"Ah, come on," I protested. "I'm just trying to—"

A large hand clapped me on the shoulder. I swiveled around to see two large goons, each wearing coveralls similar to Jose's, glaring down at me.

"You heard the boss," one of them said. "You've worn out yer welcome."

I tried to swallow, but it came out more as a scratchy gulp. Despite the soda I'd been drinking, my mouth was suddenly parched. I lifted my hands up in submission.

"Sure, sure." I slowly stood from the booth and backed away from them. "No problem. I'll leave." I started making my way toward the exit, but after a few steps I turned and looked back at Jose. "If you think of anything that might be useful, you know where to find me."

With that, I walked out of the bar and pondered my next move as I climbed back into my car.

5

Before heading back to Wonderland, I decided to head to George Trabor's house to deliver the items he'd requested for his Santa gig that night. I'd known George for a very long time. He was a quiet man, a devoted husband, and a father of three grown kids, and had been enjoying his retirement from the railroad by spreading Christmas cheer to as many children as he could for the last few decades. His house, a decent-sized ranch-style structure nestled in secluded woodland on the edge of the Ocala National Forest, was already lit up with bright red and green lights, even though the sun wasn't scheduled to descend for another three hours or so.

As I drove up the long, winding driveway, I marveled at the decorations painstakingly erected along the property. There was a full-sized sleigh with a mechanical Santa Claus at the reins and eight animatronic reindeer stamping their plastic hooves in sync with one another east of the house. To the west was a family of Styrofoam snowmen George had sculpted himself, with Christmas lights for eyes and around their top hats. A snow machine in the back yard belted out tiny particles of ice that covered George's roof. With seventy-degree weather, it was amazing that any of the snow could even take hold, but enough volume of the stuff was being pumped into the air to provide a nice snowy illusion around the property—though I shuddered to think about his water bill.

As I pulled to a stop, got out of my car, and walked around to the trunk, George opened his front door and came out to greet me.

"What do you think?" he asked, gesturing to his hard work. "It's just the beginning, mind ya. I still have a life-size manger scene and several finishing touches to bring the decorations all together."

I nodded, reached into my trunk, and pulled out the box of toys, candy canes, and bells that George had requested. "I'm impressed." I handed the box over to him and withdrew another containing a paisley-print Santa vest and two dozen child-sized T-shirts that read "Santa's Little Helper" that George liked to give to the kids. "Hard to imagine, but I think it's even more impressive than last year."

George beamed beneath his natural thick white beard. He jerked his head toward the house. "Come on inside. Got some coffee brewing, and Margaret's been wanting to see you."

Although I didn't really have time—what with the murder investigation I had decided to take on looming over me—after the day I'd had it would be nice to enjoy a little respite with old friends and a good pot of coffee. Besides, George and Margaret were some of the wisest people I knew. If anyone could help me sort this mess out, I figured they could. So I followed my old friend inside, to be greeted by a wondrous Christmas Neverland even more grandiose than outside.

The house smelled of cinnamon and baked goodies, and the sound of Christmas music played softly through Bluetooth speakers mounted in all the rooms. As we strode through the front hallway to the den, I was mesmerized by the miniature Victorian cities painstakingly created along mahogany shelves depicting a classic Dickensian Christmas-scape filled with tiny chimney sweeps, stovepipe hats, and hansom cabs. A miniature running steam engine on tiny tracks connected all the individual scenes into one grand panoramic vista.

"Your wife was always an even better decorator than you, George," I said as we entered the den. "She hasn't disappointed this year at all."

If his smile could possibly have gotten any wider, it would have. George doted on his wife, Margaret, and he often said that the only thing he'd ever done right in life was choosing her to be his bride. He credited her, as well, for the successes his children had become over the years.

"Is that Thomas Nast I hear in there?" came a delicate female voice from the direction of the kitchen. A moment later, a plump, red-faced woman in her mid-sixties strode into view, wiping her hands on her apron. Her eyes lit up when she saw me, and she immediately came over to place me in a massive bear hug. "Oh, Thomas, it's wonderful to see you again!"

"Thank you, Margaret!" My heart fluttered at the joy the woman elicited from just being in the same room with her. Being an orphan, I couldn't remember the feeling of a mother doting on me or showering me with unconditional love. And while Margaret Trabor was only a little over twenty years my elder, being in her presence was the closest thing I could imagine to what having a mother must be like. She exuded maternal nurturing to everyone she met, but I'd been fortunate enough for her to take a special interest in me over the years. To the point where she had, from her own admission, become something of a surrogate mom to me. "I'm sorry it's been a while since I came to visit," I said. "It's just..."

"Almost Christmas," she tutted. "Your busiest time of year, I know. I know. Think nothing of it, dear. I'm just glad you're here now." She gestured for me to take a seat in the armchair across from the couch. "Now, I'll be back in a few minutes with coffee and your favorite."

Her eyes twinkled. My heart skipped a beat.

"You mean..." I sat on the edge of my seat in anticipation.

She laughed. "Peanut butter pie. Just finished making it, and it's been chilling in the fridge long enough, I think."

She disappeared back into the kitchen, leaving me alone with George, who was now filling his pipe with a wad of tobacco.

"So, can you tell me what happened at the store earlier?" he asked.

I shrugged, unsure where to start. "Hank Cobb was murdered in my showroom. Stabbed so many times in the back, I couldn't count all the wounds."

Although his eyes widened just a bit, he lit the pipe, seemingly unfazed by the news. After taking a few puffs, he said, "In Wonderland? Seriously? How did *that* happen?"

"How did what happen?" Margaret asked as she came back into the den carrying a platter with three cups of coffee and three slices of peanut butter pie. She handed the plate with the largest slice over to me and winked. "You need to put some fat on those skinny bones of yours." She laughed. "Can't be Santa Claus if you're a string bean, now, can you?"

I blinked at her comment, then realized she was referring to playing the role and not about being destined to become the legend. Truth is, the *original* Santa wasn't fat either, didn't wear a red suit, and couldn't grow hair on his face to save his life. He also carried a sword, teamed up with a dwarf and a Visigoth bounty hunter, and battled a horde of goblins. But that's a tale for another time.

"Now, what were you two talking about?" Margaret asked as she sat down next to her husband.

"Hank Cobb was killed in Tom's store last night," George explained.

"Oh, how horrid! How did it happen?"

I shook my head. "That's what I'm trying to figure out. Right now, they're looking at Trixie as a suspect."

I went on to describe the events leading up to finding the body, and Trixie being taken to Orlando for questioning. I left out the part about the knife, because I wasn't sure I wanted to worry my friends that the killer might be someone they knew.

"Trixie?" Margaret's voice raised an octave as she said the name; then her brows furrowed in anger. "Well, I'll go down and tell those detectives a thing or two. That poor girl's been through enough in her life. She wouldn't hurt a fly, much less her deadbeat father...even though he might've deserved a kick in the pants every once in a while."

I smiled at the woman's faithfulness between blissful bites of the pie. I had no doubt the sweet Mrs. Trabor meant every word she said about having a word with the police in Trixie's defense. Like I said, everyone around here loved the girl and would do what was necessary to look after her. Doubly so for Margaret.

"It doesn't surprise me that he's dead, though," George said, setting his pipe down and taking a sip of his coffee. "What surprises me is just how long it took."

The revelation kind of surprised me. George was usually far more compassionate. And he and Hank had—once upon a time—been very close.

"What do you mean?" I asked. "I know the guy could be a major jerk to people, but to get someone mad enough to kill him?"

George shrugged. "Trust me. He had a lot of enemies." He

set his coffee cup down and leaned back in his seat. "Including me and Teddy Gorshon."

My eyes widened. "What?"

He glanced over at his wife, who nodded, quietly encouraging him to speak. "Well, the S.O.B. took me and Teddy for a pretty penny a few months back."

Now this *really* surprised me.

"Hank scammed you?" I couldn't believe my old friend would even consider dealing with Cobb, considering his fall from grace. Not to mention the way he'd treated Trixie for all those years. Then again, with Christmas being such a small town, I couldn't understand why anyone around here would. "How? What happened?"

George's cheeks turned three different shades of red. His wife sidled over to him and placed a reassuring arm around his shoulder.

Taking a deep breath, he sat forward on the couch to look me square in the eye. "Tom, I hope what I'm about to tell you won't seem like a betrayal or anything. It wasn't meant to be. But I've been thinking about going back to work for a while now, and couldn't think of anything I wanted to do more than..."

He hesitated. My muscles tensed. This didn't sound good at all.

"Well, Teddy Gorshon and I had planned on opening up our own holiday emporium, like yours," he finally said. "We'd thought about opening it up in Orlando, so it wouldn't directly compete with your business; but with a town named 'Christmas,' staying here just sounded too good to pass up."

Instantly, I deflated, letting out a long breath of air. Then I smiled.

"That's it?" I asked. "That's the big betrayal you were afraid to tell me?"

The older man looked over at his wife, who smiled lovingly back at him. He turned to me again.

"Well, yeah. I mean, you've been so good to me over the years. Your shop...well, let's just say I couldn't imagine anything coming close to what you and Horatio put together, but I wanted to give it a try. So did Teddy. You know how much we both love this time of year. I just didn't want you thinking we were trying to steal business away from you."

I laughed. It was a deep-throated, hearty laugh. Something I desperately needed at that moment. There was no way George could have known this, but Wonderland wasn't a business. Not in the real sense of the word. I didn't need the money. With my position, I was taken care of quite nicely, an advantage to being a Santa-in-Training. But I ran Wonderland because of the joy I had from it and a desire to feel the spirit of Christmas all year long. I knew precisely why George and Teddy had wanted to start their own shop: it was the exact same reason as me. Those two—peas in a Santa-suited pod—would be perfect for such a shop, and I honestly harbored no hard feelings at all.

I let George know that—minus the Santa destiny bit, mind you—in no uncertain terms, and I could see the instant relief on his face.

"So, what happened?" I asked. "Is your business still happening? How did Hank fit into it all?"

He scowled. "Teddy thought Hank might be able to scrape up the capital we needed to start the business." He held up his hands. "I know, I know. Stupid, right? But Hank came to us. Said he was trying to change his ways. Turn over a new leaf and all that. Said he wanted to get back into the Santa game too. Had us totally convinced he was legit, especially when he came to us saying he had a silent investor for our project. He said if we each put up twenty-five grand, his investor would make up the rest."

I rolled my eyes. "I'm assuming there was no investor."

"Oh, there was an investor, all right. The problem was that we didn't know who the investor was until we'd both forked over our share to Hank."

I sat back, waiting for George to continue.

After another puff from his pipe, he went on. "It was Vinnie Tarturo."

"The mobster?" I asked.

Everyone in Christmas knew about Vincent "Vinnie" Tarturo. He'd moved here about eight years ago from New York. There was no proof that the man was in the mafia—more rumors than anything else, based on his accent and lifestyle—but I had a fair inkling that the suspicions were pretty accurate.

George nodded. "Once we found out about his involvement, both Teddy and I wanted to back out of the deal. Hank told us we were more than welcome to do so, but that Vinnie considered our portion of the investments a handling fee for a broken deal, and that we couldn't get the money back."

"You didn't go to the police?"

"And tell them what? We gave Hank our money fair and square. He didn't take it from us. Didn't even swindle us out of it, really. And Tarturo has an army of lawyers on his speed dial; you know that."

I didn't know that, actually. I'd never had the pleasure of dealing with the man. Thank goodness. But I would take George's word on the subject.

"Instead," George continued, "we simply accepted our losses and backed out. For me, I get monthly retirement checks and

Social Security, which can easily support us. But Teddy isn't as fortunate. It cleaned him out of his savings entirely, and now the only thing he has to live on is his disability and government assistance."

"Poor Teddy."

Teddy Gorshon had had a tough few years. He was about my age, maybe a couple of years older. He'd been a farmhand in Ocala for most of his life; but in his thirties, he'd had an accident that left him disabled. He became an alcoholic. His wife left him and took his three kids. He'd been fighting for the past two years to get visitation rights for the remaining two underage children.

Thinking about Teddy's life, I could understand why he'd desperately want to believe that someone like Hank Cobb could clean up his act.

"Yeah. It's bad." George shook his head. "He hated Hank for what he did. Blamed him for losing everything."

I felt the hairs stiffen along the back of my neck.

"You don't think he'd be capable of..." I couldn't even get the words out. Teddy, despite his drinking problem, which he seemed to have kicked in recent years, was a good guy. A handyman who helped out the few local businesses around here with the occasional repair job, and he always felt guilty about asking for payment for his work.

George shrugged. "I can't imagine him..."

I cleared my throat. "George, I haven't told you everything about the murder. About the murder weapon." I proceeded to tell them about finding the knife under the body and how it was the one I'd custom-designed and given to everyone. Teddy had been one of the recipients. "So you can see why this news might worry me."

My old friend sat there for several seconds, his mouth agape. Then he clamped down on his pipe with his teeth and shook his head. "No way. No way Teddy would do anything like that. I can't believe it."

Margaret cleared her throat. "George, you need to tell Thomas what he said to you the other night. He needs to know."

"Oh, honey, that was just talk. He'd started drinking again and had gotten into one of his spells. He didn't mean it."

"Mean what?" I moved to the edge of my seat again. "What did he say, George? I need to know."

My friend closed his eyes and shook his head. "He told me he wanted to kill Hank Cobb."

6

had a lot to think about as I drove along East Colonial Drive, on my way to Comet Avenue and Wonderland. I thought about the knives. About how I'd designed them with a touch of Christmas magic. They would be forever razor-sharp. No need for whetstones or the like to hone them. I thought about how they were intended to be used as tools. Many of the recipients were avid whittlers and woodcarvers. One was an amateur toymaker. The knives were perfect for such crafts.

To use one of them as a murder weapon made no sense. There were far better instruments—butcher knives, axes, guns—to be used for murder. So, why would the killer use that particular knife?

From there, my mind turned to what I'd learned about Hank Cobb, George, and Teddy, and the deal that had left the latter nearly destitute. No one loved his kids more than Teddy. With no money, his chances of taking his wife to court for joint custody were slim to none. And while Teddy was typically an easygoing guy, I could see losing his children forever as something that might send him over the edge. I couldn't imagine Teddy murdering someone in his normal state of mind, but I hadn't talked to him in quite a while: I had no idea what his emotional state might be.

Then there was the comment about Hank trying to turn his life around. Could he truly have been trying to make things right? Could he have really been attempting to go on the straight and narrow? His dealings with the alleged gangster Vinnie Tar-turo seemed to disprove those claims, but I wasn't sure. It would certainly explain why Hank was found in a Santa suit...something he had sworn to never don again after his wife left.

By the time I unlocked the front door and tossed my coat onto a nearby armchair, my mind was awhirl with more questions than answers.

At the moment, Teddy Gorshon seemed the most likely suspect; but if I was going to play detective, I knew I needed to do it right. Including not eliminating suspects—even those like George Trabor—until I had all the facts. I prayed that George had had nothing to do with it, but the cold truth remained that he had lost a considerable sum of money to Hank as well; and while his pension and benefits from the forty years he'd worked for the railroad were considerable, he was a proud man. A staunch provider to his family. The loss of so much money over a foolish choice wouldn't have sat well with him. It was quite possible that he could have desired revenge as much as Teddy.

There had also been something about Jose, the taking-the-day-off mechanic at Stuart's Pub, that I just couldn't get out of my head. He'd been shifty in answering my questions. Nervous. He could never seem to get comfortable as we talked. And then there was the revelation that the two of them had had various business dealings with each other. Granted, he had no access to the Christmas knives, but that meant very little. If Hank had still been carrying the knife I'd given him, maybe the murder weapon had been his own.

Without looking up, still running all this information through my mind, I idled over to the cash-register counter, leaned my cane against it, and plopped down in a chair to think about my next move.

"Ahem." The cleared throat startled me out of my thoughts, and I looked up to see both Ursula Brooks and Trixie staring at me just two feet to my right. "Penny for your thoughts?"

I jumped up from my chair, ran to Trix, and wrapped my arms around her. "I'm glad you're back! I've been so worried about you!"

"I can tell." She returned the hug, patting me on the back after it became a little uncomfortable for her tough-as-nails ego. I backed away and beamed at her.

I said, "I was afraid...I was afraid they were going to charge you. I...I just didn't know what to do."

"Well, for starters, you called me," Ursula said. "That was the smartest thing you could have done."

I turned around to face my ex-girlfriend, and my jaw dropped. I'd forgotten how beautiful she was. By beauty, I'm not just referring to her physical appearance. While her long dark hair, slim figure, and tanned silky skin were certainly appealing to any man who looked at her, it was her crystal-blue eyes—like snowflakes on a pane of glass—that incongruously melted the walls I'd spent the better part of a year trying to build up. From the description of those eyes, one might get the impression that Ursula would be someone cold at heart. That her eyes would foster feelings of frostiness. An Ice Queen, perhaps. But when I say her eyes were like flakes of snow, I mean the sensation one gets from sitting back in a reading chair by a warm fire surrounded by your dearest family and friends. Her beauty came from the warmth of her soul. The ease at which she could offer a smile, or nurture one in return. If the eyes were a reflection of the soul, hers shone brightly, showing that she was quick to laugh, easy to love, and determined when it came to taking care of those she held dear.

I'd forgotten that about her, which was exactly the point of trying to avoid her all this time.

My heart nearly tore in two all over again as I gazed at her, remembering that awful night I'd revealed my secret to her. Her reaction. Her panic and doubt. It had been the worst night of my life; and now, seeing her, I was drumming it up all over again.

Trixie, who was aware of what had happened between us, placed a hand on my shoulder for support. To calm me.

It worked.

"Ursula," I said with a nod. "It's good to see you again."

She smiled, but there was no sign of her characteristic warmth in it. I had, after all, broken her heart too, though she could not remember why.

"Is it? I figured you'd want to get as far away from me as possible, considering the way you've been acting lately."

I didn't even want to consider how flushed my face was because of her comment, so I averted my eyes a millisecond later and turned back to Trixie without replying.

"So, are you okay?" I asked her.

She shrugged. "As good as can be expected. Ursula says I'm still a suspect, but it was easier for them to release me and charge me later as they build up a case. So I'm not sure how I feel, exactly."

"I meant about your father. The case will take care of itself. I want to know how you're feeling about your dad."

Her face was still streaked with the black lines of her mascara, but her cheeks and eyes were dry now. Her lips tightened in a look of quiet strength. "He was never my dad," she said. "Father, yes. But never my dad. To be honest, I'm about as upset over his death as I would be over anyone's."

That was significant in its own right. Despite her tough exterior, Trixie wore her heart on her sleeve. She was wildly empathetic. She cared about everyone, which is why so many people who knew her cared just as much about her. She was one of the most compassionate people I'd ever met, a young woman who tended to become quite upset each night over the evening news.

"I'm so sorry," I told her, bringing her into another hug and stroking her hair.

She sniffed, then backed away, wiping a fresh set of tears from her eyes. "I'll be all right. I've got you and Pep." She smiled at this, and I gave her a wink.

"Pep again?" Ursula said. She'd heard us talk about Peppermint a number of times in the past, and we'd played him off as an inside joke between the two of us. But now was no time to get caught up in that discussion again, so I decided to steer our conversation toward something more productive.

Taking a seat in my armchair, I crossed my legs and motioned for them to take the chairs across from me, near one of the smaller Christmas trees on display. When they did, I cleared my throat and began asking the questions I'd been holding on to since first discovering the body this morning.

"Can you tell me what happened last night, Trix?"

Her head lolled over the back of her chair, and she let out a frustrated groan. She'd probably already repeated this story a hundred times, so I'm sure she was getting tired of reliving it. Ursula gave me a stern, protective look that confirmed my suspicions. But I needed to understand. I needed the facts if I was going to help her.

"Come on, Trixie. I just need you to go over it one more time. The last time, I promise."

She lifted her head and rolled her eyes at me. "Okay. Fine." Her right leg hopped nervously up and down as she spoke. "Seth and I went to Stuart's last night after studying."

"I know about that. Don't need those details." I really didn't like Seth Timmons much at all. "Just get to the part where you and your father had the confrontation."

Trixie nodded, then swallowed. "I guess it was around midnight. Seth had already headed home. Because of how stressed I was over the exam—which I missed, by the way, because of all this—I decided to stay a while longer and just unwind a bit more."

I knew, to her, unwinding "a bit more" could be a kick-to-the-head-ton of booze to other people, but I didn't say anything. She didn't need my disapproval now. She needed my steadfast support.

"Anyway, I was just about to leave when Hanky came in wearing that ridiculous old Santa outfit of his." Trixie had called her dad "Hanky" since she was a little girl. She'd grown up hearing people call him by his first name and couldn't reconcile it with the name "Daddy," so she'd simply combined the two. Neither parent had bothered to correct her. "For a minute, I didn't recognize him. He looked sober. And I had been too young to remember him ever dressing up as Santa. But the moment he saw me, our eyes locked and I knew who he was. He made a beeline toward me, and I figured he was there to ask me for money for booze, so I got up and started heading to the door."

She coughed, tried to clear her throat, and coughed again. I figured her throat must have been parched from talking all morning to the police. As I thought about that, an antique end table slid silently across the floor to her, but out of view from

Ursula. Trixie noticed, lowered her hand, and brought up a large glass of crystal-clear water. She took a deep gulp. If my ex noticed, she didn't show it, continuing to keep her gaze on her client. I had no doubt she'd heard all this before—probably in the interrogation room with the cops—but her keen mind would be listening to any variations in detail that might be exploited by prosecutors.

"Go on, Trixie," she said. "Tell him what happened next."

Taking another gulp of water, Trix set the glass down on the table and continued. "Hanky followed me outside. I tried to get away, but he caught up with me, tossed a duffel bag on the ground, and grabbed my arm. He said he'd changed. That he was working on his drinking, and that he had just come into some real money and was going to leave town and start a new life."

I wondered if he was talking about the money he'd swindled George and Teddy out of, but fifty grand wasn't exactly something to brag about these days. I mean, it was a lot for someone like Hank, but it wasn't exactly "start a new life" money. Or, at least, it wouldn't get him very far.

"The weird thing is, he wanted *me* to go with him," she said. "He said he wanted to try to work things out with me. To be my dad again."

I blinked. It matched up with what Hank had told George, but it was so hard to believe. We had all pretty much written the man off as lost. Could he really have been trying to change?

"What did you say to that?"

"I laughed in his face. Told him there was no way on Earth I'd ever give him a chance again." She paused, obviously reflecting on the incident with some regret. "That made him mad. He started shaking me at that point; and I was so drunk, I slipped and fell."

"So, he didn't push you down?"

She shook her head. "I don't know where that came from. I was just really unsteady. Sure, he'd gotten a little rough, but nowhere near what he used to get with me. In fact, he was really restrained. It was kind of weird."

"Do you think he was serious about trying to change? About wanting to reconcile with you?"

"I don't know. Maybe." She blinked back a tear and wiped it away with a finger. "But I wasn't going to give him the chance. I started running. I'd already planned to come back here and sleep in…" She glanced over at Ursula and cleared her throat. She had to be careful what she said next, and she was well aware of it. "…in the guest room downstairs."

The guest room she was referring to was her sanctum sanctorum nestled somewhere in the labyrinthine walls of the House. It was her own place of refuge that the House had created exclusively for her.

"Wait," I said. "I thought you assaulted him too. That's what the witness told the police."

She shook her head. "A complete lie. All I wanted to do was get away from him. Hanky and I have fought tooth and nail my whole life. We've both put each other in the hospital several times. And frankly, I was tired of it. I wasn't angry with him. I wasn't all that upset, really. I just didn't want to deal with his BS anymore. So I ran."

This wasn't tracking at all with what Jose Jimenez had told me at the pub earlier. He'd made it sound like Trixie had been a raving lunatic bent on maiming or killing Hank Cobb right there on the spot. And while one of them could be lying, I trusted Trixie enough to put my money on her telling the truth.

"You came straight here?"

She nodded. "Ran inside." She looked up at me, her lips jutting slightly. "I'm sorry, Tom. I must have left the door wide open in my hurry to get away from him. I figure he followed me inside; but by the time he did, I was already in the..." She glanced at Ursula. "...guest room."

"And after you got there, when Hank came inside looking for you, someone else followed him in and killed him."

"That's the way it sounds to me too," Ursula said. "But something I don't understand, sweetie. When the police found you, you weren't in a room. They told me they found you along one of the corridors, passed out on a pile of holly? That the berries had been crushed under your weight, and you were covered in juice?"

Trixie looked over at me with pleading eyes. I knew what she was silently asking me. Like I said earlier, Trixie's room is very special, and like many other places in the house, intruders are not welcome to witness everything the way it actually is. Having never been to her specially prepared haven, I wasn't sure what she'd been lying on, but it would have been something very special to her. Something comfortable, and specifically designed to offer her a deep sense of well-being. But to the casual observer, the House would cloud their minds to see any number of things. The fact that it had chosen holly bushes was an interesting touch. But the question was, how could we explain all that to Ursula?

I was just about to offer a reasonable explanation for the discrepancy when Ursula's phone rang. She glanced down to see who was calling, and her nose wrinkled. "Ah, for crying out loud." She looked at me. "It's Janet. I swear, sometimes it seems like I can't be away more than fifteen minutes without her calling me about something." She stood, answered her phone, and stepped away from the two of us.

"That was a close one," Trixie said.

"Eh, it would have been okay. She knows how wonky this place can be. We could have come up with a reasonable excuse if we'd needed to."

"Well, I wish you'd get that woman out of here," said a new voice, which caused both of us to jump. "She's a plague. A harpy. A genuine scourge upon my calm."

Trix burst into a smile. "Pep!" she whispered. Trix and Peppermint had a special relationship. A conspiracy at times, I suspected. They were the best of friends, so I knew she'd be happy to have him lurking around now. "I'm glad you're here," she whispered to him.

"Of course. I just wish I could have stopped those buffoonish constables from carting you off to the pokey." The elf let out a low growl. "But Beanpole here wouldn't have appreciated my interference."

The Beanpole he was referring to, I knew, was me.

"Pep, you didn't see anything last night?" Trixie asked. She glanced around the floor, trying to pinpoint precisely where he was, even though she knew it would be impossible.

"I'm sorry, love. Hit the bourbon a little too hard last night." He giggled. "Something else we 'ave in common, eh? But alas, no. Didn't see a thing." From his tone of voice, I could tell he was sincerely contrite about that fact, so I'd forgo my inclination to give him a lecture later about his drinking. If he had to do it all over again, I knew he would have remained sober to protect Trix. It didn't mean it wouldn't happen again, but at least for now he was mortified at his failure.

"Well, I need to go," Ursula said, as she slipped her phone into her purse and walked back over to us. "Janet just told me that one of our clients is freaking out about an upcoming hearing and needs me to come hold his hand." She approached Trixie, bent down, and kissed her on the forehead. "Don't worry, sweetie. We'll get this all sorted out, I promise."

Trixie nodded and mouthed a "thank you" to her.

Turning to me, Ursula said, "Let me know if anything else happens. We need to stay ahead of the cops on this. Be sure to head off any problems before they happen."

"I'll keep poking around," I told her, then tried to swallow past my parched throat. "It really was good to see you again."

She smiled back at me with a tilt of her head that told me she was in agreement but not ready to verbally state it, before walking out of the store.

7

woke up the next morning feeling as though I hadn't closed my eyes at all. My muscles ached, but not nearly as much as the area between my temples, which throbbed with one humdinger of a stress-induced migraine. The moment I opened my eyes, I shivered in my Victorian-era sleigh bed, nestled so comfortably in my comforter that I loathed the thought of moving. It was a new day, but the problems of yesterday still lingered in the forefront of my mind like a tangle of eyelashes that just won't go away.

It was also spectacularly cold in my room, which made getting up that much harder. I wasn't sure what temperature I had the air conditioning set to. Normally, I kept the house at a steady, and comfortable, seventy-two degrees Fahrenheit throughout the year, but the frigid air biting at my nose and forehead peeking out above the covers seemed much colder than that.

Besides being puzzled over the temperature, I also wondered what time it was, but was too tired—and too cold—to even turn my head to look at the clock. From the grim amount of light seeping through the curtains at my window, I figured it was approaching dawn, and contemplated whether I should roll over and get a few more hours of sleep before the store opened. It took less than a minute to decide that that was the best course of action, so I shifted onto my side to keep the approaching daylight from waking me again prematurely, pulled my blanket up to my neck, and closed my eyes again with a determined smile on my face.

The problems would still be there when I woke up. They weren't going anywhere. So, what would it hurt to just push them from my mind a little while longer?

"Um, what's going on, Santa's Little Dum-dum?" came a high-pitched British-accented voice from somewhere behind me. "It's snowing in your bedroom."

My eyes blinked open, but I still nuzzled my head against my pillow. "Knock it off," I mumbled. "I'm in no mood for your games."

"Well, as much as I'd love to take credit for it, this is no prank. If you'd bother to open your eyes, you'd see that, indeed, it *is* snowing. In *your* bedroom. And no matter what slanderous accusations you might hurl my way, I had nothing to do with it."

I rubbed at my eyes, but it was still so dark in my room that I couldn't see clearly.

"It's still early. Sun's not even fully up yet," I grumbled, no longer having energy enough to care whether it had snowed or if this was one of Peppermint's regular attempts to rile me.

"It's not early. In fact, you're late for work, and Trixie's got her hands full with customers." My comforter and sheets were yanked viciously from me and flew onto the floor. "The sun's definitely up. Just covered by some mighty nasty clouds." Peppermint paused. "And a few snow flurries outside to boot."

I jerked up in my bed. Snow? Yesterday, the high had been seventy-eight degrees. The weather forecast for today said it was supposed to reach the low eighties. Now there's snow?

I blinked as I gazed around my room. The floor, as well as the blankets that now lay in a pile next to the bed, were covered in a fine layer of white powder.

...the heck?

It really had snowed in my room last night. But that's...that's crazy.

I swung my legs around and placed my feet on the Persian rug—now icy with snowflakes—beneath my bed.

"That can't be right. How did it snow in my room?"

"Tick-tock, Beanpole," Peppermint said. "That's something to figure out later. Like I said, you're late for work, and the store is packed with customers. Trix needs help."

I was still focused on the snow, but I turned to my nightstand and looked at my alarm clock. It was 9:42 am.

"What?" I bolted from the bed and threw open the curtains. Sure enough, the sky was gray. Overcast. And while I couldn't see any snow outside, the extreme low temperature nearly radiated from the windowpane.

"Whatever you're doing, you better stop it," Peppermint said. "Snow in Florida isn't unprecedented, but it's not normal either. Snow inside a building, though...now, that's bordering on the absurd."

I shook my head. "It's just my room. No one will notice."

Pep chuckled. "I've got news for you, pal: it's snowing downstairs too. The House is loving it, by the way. It's tickled pink by the stuff."

My eyes widened. "It's snowing downstairs? Now?"

"Yup. So you better knock it off before anyone wises up to you."

"But I'm not doing this." I whirled around, looking for the little elf. "This can't be me."

"Of course it is. Next in line to Krin'Ghal's throne. The weather can get a little weird when your emotions get out of whack, and I'd say, after yesterday, your emotions are about as catawampus as they can get." The door to my walk-in closet opened, and a minute later the invisible Pep tossed a freshly pressed suit on my bed, followed by a bright red bowler hat. "Now get dressed. Trixie's in no condition to handle those blokes downstairs on her own."

Ten minutes later, cane in hand, I descended the spiral staircase to my showroom floor and instantly knew that Peppermint had been right. The place was packed. With Christmas just eight days away, and because my store had been closed all day yesterday, the place was a madhouse filled with would-be Santas, a half-dozen tourists just browsing the shop's novelties, and a proverbial murder of cawing moms looking for the perfect Christmas present for their little bundles of joy. I cringed, anticipating the irritated mob of stressed-out shoppers, but as I drew nearer, I noticed something amazing.

The customers were overjoyed. Happy. Having the time of their lives.

And it was all, I believed, thanks to the light flutter of snowflakes drifting throughout the store as Bing Crosby belted out "White Christmas" over the store's ceiling-mounted speakers.

Intrigued, I watched as my customers marveled at the falling snow. Their gazes stretched up to the domed ceiling, where a haze of fog gathered like balls of gray cotton, releasing its crystalline prize to the world below. The children, most of whom had never seen snow in real life, stuck out their tongues to catch the falling flakes. Older women and wrinkled gentlemen giggled as much as the kids, watching the snow in awe as if reliving the simpler times of their youth.

I had to admit it was rather breathtaking, despite much of my merchandise now being covered with a thin veil of frozen moisture, which would melt eventually. It would be a mess to clean up, but then I'd let the House take care of all that later. For now, despite yesterday's concerns still bearing down on me, I'd accept the phenomenon for what it was—a miracle to be enjoyed.

The moment my feet touched the first floor, I was bombarded by customers, commending me for my wonderful Christmas decoration.

"It's truly marvelous," one grandmotherly woman told me, smiling from ear to ear.

"Ol' George Trabor's got to step up his game if he wants to compete with real snow in his decorations," Jeremy Gilmour told me, chuckling as he walked past.

One of the children, a young boy who'd been coming to Wonderland since he'd still been in diapers, stared wide-eyed at the apparition. "How did you do this, Mr. Nast? How did you get it to snow?"

It was times such as these that I got the sense that, one day, I really *would* like kids. Their sense of wonder and joy over the simplest thing was inspiring, and this boy's gawking giddiness was worth the wet mess we would have to endure once the magic had run its course.

The day moved fast. More and more customers came in to see the amazing spectacle, with no one suspecting that it was anything more than a Christmas gimmick. I let them think that, as I weaved my way through the throng helping the half-crazed, half-mesmerized customers as fast as I could.

For her part, Trixie was running the register like a pro—all business—and didn't seem the least bit fazed by the busy morning or the sudden climate change. I suppose the chaos was a reprieve from the madness of the last twenty-four hours, but it reminded me that I needed to give the poor girl a much-deserved raise whenever I could get around to it.

"This snow is amazing," someone behind me said.

Startled, I turned around to see Eli Smart. A tall, lanky kid of about eighteen. His dad, Jonathan Smart, had been a regular customer and a great department-store Santa in his day. He'd also been one of the six who had received a pocketknife from me. Unfortunately, he'd passed away two years earlier from pancreatic cancer. Wanting to honor his father, Eli had started playing Santa at various elementary schools in the area—at least until the schools let out for Christmas break.

"Using a bit of your Christmas magic?" he asked with a wink.

He also believed I was the *real* Santa Claus for some reason. I wasn't sure if he'd seen one too many strange things at Wonderland or simply had an intuition others didn't, but he'd pretty much insisted I was Santa since he was around seven years old.

It hadn't really bothered me until his dad got sick and Eli pleaded with me to use my "magic" to make him better. It was one gift I could never have given, even if I was indeed Santa. The Christmas Spirit has no power over life or death.

"Eli, how many times do I have to tell you—"

He smiled, holding up his hands. "I know. I know. You're not *really* Santa Claus." He shot me another wink, then suddenly became serious. "Heard you had a crazy day yesterday."

"You heard about that, eh?"

"Everyone has," he said, nodding over to Trixie. "Everyone's dying to talk to her about it, but ya know...no one wants to bring up bad feelings around her. They're all being real careful."

"I'm glad. Last thing she needs right now is a reminder of yesterday."

I liked Eli. He was a good kid and had had a serious crush on Trixie for the past two and a half years. If it wasn't for his little bout of underage drinking that started when his dad died, and if Eli had been a couple of years older, I would have wholeheartedly endorsed him and Trix getting together. After all, I'd much prefer her to hang out with him than that loathsome ne'er-do-well Seth Timmons.

"So, can I help you find something today, Eli?" I asked. He wasn't holding any merchandise, instead simply standing uncomfortably close to me, staring awkwardly at Trixie like a cartoon wolf with its tongue lolling out to the floor. It was making me uncomfortable.

"Nah," he said. "I was supposed to be working on Mrs. O'Hare's lawn, but..." He nodded toward the front of the store. "It's snowing and stuff. Not just in here. Outside too!" He shook his head. "Crazy, huh? Actual snow. In Central Florida. Not much. Just a little dusting, but enough that I got the day off."

I cringed at the mention of the weather outside. It was one thing to offer some winter weather inside the shop. There were other Christmas-themed stores that did that year-round. But outside? In Florida? I was afraid Peppermint was right, and my anxiety over Hank Cobb's murder—and Trixie being the prime suspect—was going to be a problem. This kind of thing had happened to me once before, though it hadn't been nearly as dramatic a change as this. And it hadn't been at such a critical time.

Given Eli's own suspicions of my connection to Christmas, I decided to steer the subject away to something a little more manageable.

"I forgot you were helping out at Mallory O'Hare's estate," I told him. Actually, it had been court-ordered after a little drinking-and-driving incident during the summer. The judge had thought that a part-time job like tending lawns—as well as seeking professional help for his alcohol dependence—was punishment enough. "What's that been like?"

Mallory O'Hare. Now there was a thorn in my side if there ever was one. She would no doubt be the first to blame me for the strange weather we were having, no matter how crazy it might sound to others.

She was old money from an old family that had practically run the town of Christmas since the colonial days when it had been little more than a wooden fort to fend off the Seminole. In her mind, she was queen of all she surveyed and had been working nonstop for the past decade to incorporate the town into a real city with a real government with herself as the *de facto* mayor. On top of it all, she despised the touristy lure that a town named Christmas drew, and saw the Christmas-themed businesses, such as my own, as tacky and undesired. She'd made it clear on more than one occasion that, once she'd secured the support necessary to incorporate, the town's name would be changed, and I would be run out of here faster than I could say "Ho ho ho."

Eli laughed at the question. "You know exactly what it's been like," he said. "But it's not like I had any better options. Besides, she gives me some cash here and there…under the table, of course. I'm saving for college next year, so I can handle her hoity-toity nagging all day as long as her checks keep clearing."

I nodded at this, unsure of what else to say. Fortunately, I didn't have to think long. He cleared his throat.

"Um, speaking of Mrs. O'Hare, there's something I think you should know." That didn't sound good. Usually when someone told me I needed to know something about Mallory, it had something to do with Wonderland and her quest to bring it to ruin. I turned my attention away from a couple of older gentlemen in the fake-beard section and looked at Eli. "I know you're looking into Mr. Cobb's murder," he said. News does travel fast around here. "Well, anyway, I was at her house a couple of days ago. Mr. Cobb came by to talk with her."

My ears perked up at this. "Really? What did they talk about?"

Eli shook his head. "Not sure exactly. I was outside working in the garden, so I only caught bits and pieces through an open window. I heard him mention Vinnie Tarturo and something about needing money. Something about if she did this one thing, Ms. Mallory would never see him again. That he was leaving town and taking Trixie with him." He paused. "Then the maintenance man came by with a leaf blower and I couldn't hear anything else. But by the end of the conversation, Mrs. O'Hare was screaming at Mr. Cobb. Called him every bad word in the book and told him to leave. She said if he ever came to her house again, she'd shoot him and wouldn't think twice about it." The boy let out a soft chuckle. "I've never seen that man run so fast—and in such a straight line—in my life. He ran out of the house, hopped in that old van of his, and hightailed it out of there fast. Never looked back once."

Now, *that* was an interesting little tidbit. I added Mallory to my mental list of the people I needed to talk to as I continued my investigation. I thanked Eli for the info and left him to resume his star-struck gaze at Trixie.

I walked over to the counter to see how she was holding up, and whether she needed a break. As I did, the bell above the door jingled, and a frigid wind blew in. The snow inside the store swirled about, like a spiral of white dust. I looked up to see Detective Tice's grim face marching up to the counter with his eyes locked dangerously on me.

"I think you and I need to have a little chat," he said, a large vein protruding from his forehead.

And I think I'm going to need a drink before this day is done, I thought while motioning the detective to follow me toward the back of the house and the solitude of the kitchen.

8

When we entered the kitchen, I was relieved to see it wasn't snowing, though a few traces could be seen along the countertop. I directed Tice to take a seat at an old ice-cream-parlor table before walking over to the cabinets and pulling out two mugs, a kettle, and cinnamon-spiced tea. I set to work preparing it, motioning for the detective to proceed.

"Neat trick with the snow," he said while I lit the gas stove and set the kettle of water on the flame. "How are you doing it?"

I shrugged, keeping my back turned to him as I pulled out some sugar, cream, and other necessities for the tea. "Shaved-ice chips blown through the ventilation," I lied. "Not too hard to pull off with a little imagination." I turned to look at him while I waited for the kettle to boil. "So, you have some questions for me, Detective?"

He leaned back in the kitchen chair, his large frame causing the legs to creak, and pulled a small notebook and a digital recorder from his jacket pocket. "You mind if I record this?" he asked.

"Not at all," I said, and he pressed the red button on the side of the device. He cleared his throat and spoke.

"Mr. Nast, you and I have a bit of a problem."

That was a heck of a way to start an interview. There was no question in it. But I figured it was a good way for the detective to get an early start at establishing dominance in our exchange. I struggled not to react, and instead pursed my lips with a nod, and motioned for him to continue.

"See, Jose Jimenez wasn't exactly happy you came to see him yesterday. Said you were harassing him. Butting your nose in where it didn't belong. Said you were asking around about Hank Cobb and the murder, and that's an issue for me."

I wasn't sure I liked the tone in his voice. I could understand why he might not like me investigating the murder, but the way he'd just spoken to me was...well, patronizing. Like he was dressing down a school kid on the playground or something. My hackles were raised, and I took a deep breath to avoid losing my cool, which would be another surefire way for him to gain the upper hand in our conversation.

"I'm not sure I understand the problem," I told him. "As a private citizen, I believe I have the right to make any inquiries I would like, as long as it doesn't hamper your investigation."

"Now, see, that's what I'm talking about right there. It *is* a problem."

The high-pitched squeal of the kettle announced that the water was ready to be poured. I held up a hand to silence him—my own attempt at establishing control—and poured the water into the mugs before taking a moment to steep the bags. I then took his mug over to him and set it down in front of him.

"Cream? Sugar?"

He shook his head "no," and I moved back to the counter to finish preparing my own cup. When I finished, I took a seat across from him and nodded at him to continue.

Clearly irritated, he grimaced before taking a sip of the tea.

"See," he finally said, wiping away a stray drop of tea from his chin with his shirt sleeve. "I haven't cleared anyone of this crime yet. I might have been looking at your employee for it yesterday, but that doesn't mean she's my only suspect."

My eyes widened. "Me? You think I'm a suspect?"

"The knife used to kill our victim was one of your own custom jobs."

I laughed at how preposterous that sounded, and he moved on.

"You also had something to gain from Cobb's death."

"Like what?"

He smiled. It was the slick, venomous, sliver-like lips of a snake.

"I know you're aware that Cobb was working with..." He glanced down at his notes. "...a Mr. George Trabor and Theodore Gorshon to open a competing store in the area. Mr. Trabor told me he'd admitted that much to you yesterday, when you were conducting your little investigation."

"Yeah, but—"

"But neither Trabor or Gorshon had the contacts or revenue stream to make that happen," Tice pushed. "Hank Cobb was facilitating a deal with an investor that would offer the capital to build their dream. A dream that would cut into whatever meager profits this place provides you."

"Okay, but I—"

"It was just icing on the cake that Cobb was the father of the girl you'd taken in a couple of years ago. A man who had relentlessly beaten and demoralized her throughout her life and driven her to such a dark place." He paused. "I can see that you care for Ms. McNamara a great deal. I could see that yesterday when we led her away in handcuffs. But at the time, you must have thought it was a golden opportunity to kill Cobb. Two birds with one stone, so to speak."

"Can I—"

"What I don't understand is that you seem like a reasonably smart guy. I can't for the life of me think why you'd be so stupid as to kill the guy in your own place, then call the police." He laughed. "I mean, that's just really dumb."

I felt the floor underneath us rumble. I could hear the timbers in the walls creaking like trees on a windy day.

Oh, crap.

"Detective, you really should—"

"I'm not finished yet!" His face was beet-red. "Way I see it, you think us cops are a bunch of idiots. You're one of those guys who thinks you're so much smarter than everyone else. One of those killers who likes to play games with the police, and I'm not having it."

The teacups trembled within their saucers as the House's foundation rattled again. But the detective didn't seem to notice. He was too far in the zone. Too far into making connections that weren't there and sizing me up for a striped prison uniform before I'd even had a trial.

And the House didn't like it.

It rumbled again, sending plates, cups, and knickknacks tumbling from their perches and crashing to the floor. The overhead lights flickered wildly, and there was a deep human-like moan that belched from the building's foundation.

"And if you are the killer, don't think for a second that I won't catch... Wait a minute. What the heck is going on?" Tice said, finally noticing the chaos around him.

Then there was a rending sound of metal, and one wrought-iron leg of the chair he was sitting on twisted out of place and snapped. The detective fell backward onto the floor, and the House fell silent.

Funny thing was, I knew the people in the store had probably not felt or heard a thing. This little show was for the detective's benefit and no one else. The House—who felt differently about me than Peppermint—didn't appreciate the way Tice had been treating its master and wanted him to know it.

Scrambling over to the big man, I reached down to help him to his feet.

"What just happened?" he asked, rubbing the back of his head where he must have struck it on the tile floor when he fell.

I looked around in mock confusion. "I've no idea. An earthquake, maybe?"

"In Florida?" He stared down at the now-three-legged chair he'd been sitting on. His mouth gaped open, unable to grasp the chain of events that had sent him spiraling to the floor.

"It's been snowing, too," I said. "Some weird weather. Maybe it's connected?"

The cop dusted himself off, adjusted his tie, and ran his fingers through his thinning hair to straighten it out. "Uh, maybe," he said, looking around the room as if ready for it to collapse on his head.

"Plus, it's a really old house. The cold weather might just be making it settle. Probably nothing to worry about."

He was now backing toward the kitchen door. "Yeah, that's probably it."

The man's earlier bravado had deflated. He moved as if the floor underneath him might open and swallow him whole. He didn't know that that was a distinct possibility, but the House wasn't evil. It wasn't haunted. It was, in truth, filled with the spirit of Christmas just as much as Krin'Ghal. Just as much as I would one day be. Which means that it had nothing but goodwill toward people in general. It could be angered. It could lash out to protect those it cared about. But it would never intentionally harm someone.

Detective Tice shook his head, as if clearing his thoughts, then he glared at me once more. "You've been warned, Nast," he said with a scowl. "If you killed Cobb, I'll find out. If that Goth delinquent did it, I'll find that out too. I don't need you butting your nose into my investigation. If I find out you're questioning any more people, I'll arrest you for tampering with an official police investigation."

The moment he said this, the room began to shake again. With eyes as large as the saucers now broken on my kitchen floor, he backed out through the door and disappeared from sight.

Peppermint burst out in uproarious laughter the moment the door closed behind the detective. "Did you see the look on that copper's face? Hahahaha! Priceless!"

I looked in the direction of his voice and glared. "It's not funny." Well, it kind of was, but I couldn't let him or the House know that. It would mean anarchy whenever those two decided they didn't particularly like someone. "This is serious. Now Trixie and I both are suspects."

"Ah, come on, Beanpole. There's no way he thinks you're a suspect. Not really. If you were, why would he be giving you such lip about your investigation? A killer doesn't investigate his own murder, now, does he?" The elf was still chuckling. "He was just trying to make you sweat. That's all."

"Well," I said as I made my way back into the store, "it worked marvelously."

9

I pulled the T-Bird up to the corner of Yule and Mistletoe Lanes and put it in park before pulling a piece of paper from my shirt pocket and unfolding it. Fortunately, after the crowd died down at Wonderland and the sun began to set, it had stopped snowing and the temperature had gradually grown to an almost balmy forty-three degrees. Still, it was cool enough in a ragtop convertible that I had to crank up the car's heater before I glanced at the list scrawled across the paper.

The list contained six names. Names of those I'd given the knives to all those years ago. I didn't want to even consider the possibility of any one of them committing murder, but let's face it: they were the most likely candidates for suspects I could hope to find. If I was going to do this investigation right, I needed to start with them. I figured it would be a relatively simple matter. Find which of them no longer had their pocketknife, and I'd also most likely have found the killer. That is, if any of them had actually done it.

After all, the knife that killed Hank Cobb could just as easily have been his own. I had no idea if he'd even kept it, but it was a definite possibility. Despite the pros or cons of my logic, I figured this was the most reasonable place to start.

The List.

I glanced down at the paper before realizing it was already

too dark to read. I reached into my jacket pocket, pulled out a penlight, and shone it on the page.

George Trabor
Hank Cobb
~~Jonathan Smart~~
Teddy Gorshon
Alphonso Garcia
Bill Sweeney

I'd already scratched Jonathan Smart's name from the list, given that he was now deceased and the least likely to be an actual suspect in the murder. I'd already spoken with George, but hadn't yet really questioned him about the whereabouts of his own knife. But when deciding which of my oldest friends to question first, I decided the best approach—so as to not play favorites and to keep an unbiased, level head—was to start geographically closest to Wonderland and make my way outward.

That meant Alphonso Garcia—our town's one and only Cuban Santa Claus and the owner/proprietor of Sleighbell Lanes bowling alley—was the first on the list.

I looked up from the page and glanced across the street to Al's modest mid-century home that looked nearly identical to every other house on the block. With one key difference. While all the other houses had made a worthwhile attempt at yuletide decorating, Al and Cindy Garcia's home practically radiated with Christmas spirit. A full-sized manger scene sat front and center on the lawn, complete with a glowing angel that seemed to hover above it all on a near-invisible zipline that whirled him around the sky every few minutes. On the other side of the walkway leading to the front door, near the old live oak whose branches drooped into the soil from age and weight, stood giant inflatable Santa Clauses, snowmen, and reindeer, along with row after row of flashing white lights clustered in every tree, shrub, and gutter on the property.

It was nothing compared to George Trabor's place, but given Al's meager means and small parcel of property to work with, it was all the more impressive. Besides, Christmas wasn't a competition. What mattered to me more was the spirit in which the decorations were displayed, and Al and Cindy had spirit enough to spare.

I folded the paper up again and tucked it back into my shirt pocket before climbing out of the car and jogging up to the front door. Pressing the doorbell, I was greeted by the sound of bells chiming the tune of "Santa Claus Is Coming to Town."

After the three Great Danes inside had stopped barking from the festive chime, and the four children between ages two and eleven had settled down enough from the excitement of visitors at the door, I heard large bare feet thudding against the linoleum floors from the atrium beyond. There was a brief pause, then the curtain covering the half-moon window parted to the left and a bright brown eye peered at me from the other side of the door. A second later, recognition and a booming laugh echoed from inside the house just as the door swung open to reveal a great bear of a man.

Seriously. Alphonso could easily have doubled for Ben, the bear on TV's *The Life and Times of Grizzly Adams*, if the need had arisen. Standing about six feet tall, he was a few inches shorter than me but was about half as wide as he was tall. The man was easily four hundred pounds, though I suspected much of it was muscle underneath layers of fat. His face sported a thick moustache and beard that hung down past his chest and was now colored white for the season. There wasn't a follicle of hair on top of his head, though, which he typically kept covered with a tweed scally cap.

"As I live and breathe," he said, beaming from ear to ear. His Cuban accent still remained thick despite having lived in the United States for nearly thirty years. "Tom Nast! What brings ya to my neck of the woods?"

I smiled back at him, shaking his proffered hand. Cindy Garcia stepped into view, holding her two-year-old girl with one hand and an eggbeater covered in cake icing with the other. She gave me a welcome nod and I waved back in greeting. I could hear the other children toward the other end of the house playing. The Great Danes, thankfully, had most likely been taken to one of the bedrooms before the door was even opened.

Don't get me wrong. I love dogs. But three canines of my mass or more, full of drool, slobber, and sledgehammers for wagging tails, were not always a welcome sight. Especially considering the business that had brought me here.

"Hey, Al," I said. "Listen, I was hoping we could chat for a bit, if that's okay."

The big man stepped aside and gestured for me to enter his home. Wiping my feet on the rug, I followed my friend from the foyer into the den. As expected, the entire room sported classic family Christmas decorations. A wonderfully trimmed live Christmas tree, with a toy train set around the base. Colorful bulbs blinked on and off, illuminating the myriad of wooden toys, used as ornaments, hanging from its boughs. And a heap of carefully wrapped presents sat against the tree within the perimeter of the train tracks.

I glanced over at the fireplace where all the kids' stockings— hand-sewn by Cindy herself—hung ready for a visit from jolly ol' St. Nick.

Al gestured to the couch. "Take a load off."

I did, and he eased himself into the La-Z-Boy across from me. Cindy disappeared into the kitchen, where I suspected she was preparing something for us to drink.

"What can I do for you, Tom?" His face was suddenly serious. I figured he could guess what this was about.

"You heard about Hank?"

He scowled, then nodded. His normally sparkling eyes dulled for a moment as if in thought. Of us all, Al had been closest to Hank Cobb in the good old days. They'd been thick as thieves. Before Al had met and married Cindy, he'd spent many a Christmas at the Cobbs' home as part of the family.

"Not many people in town haven't heard about it." He sniffed. "How's Tricia doing?"

Having spent a great deal of time with Trix as a baby—bonding with her as a kind of uncle—he'd never been comfortable calling her by her chosen nickname. He insisted on using her given name of Patricia, or simply Tricia.

I shrugged. "She's coping. Not only is she a prime suspect in the murder, but I think she's struggling to deal with the death of her dad."

"I can imagine. Poor thing." He sighed. "Let her know she can talk to me anytime. I want to be there for her if I can."

"She knows that, Al. You've always been there for her; even more than me, really."

Cindy stepped back into the living room holding two glasses of eggnog and set one in front of me on the coffee table. She handed the other to her husband, then wandered back into the kitchen without a word.

I took a sip of nog, savoring the semi-sweet taste as it ran down my throat. There was no alcohol in it—Al was a recovering alcoholic, from before I even met him, and steered clear of the stuff—but the gentle tang of ginger ale helped give the drink just enough kick to hit the spot.

"Look, Al, I'm just going to come right out and ask," I said after setting the glass on a coaster. "Please don't take this personally. I'm going to be asking everyone."

His eyes narrowed ever so slightly, but he nodded his understanding.

"Remember that Swiss Army knife I gave you about fifteen years ago?"

He cocked his head to one side, obviously confused by the question. "The knife?"

I pursed my lips together, trying to figure out the best tack to approach this on without giving too much away about the murder itself. In the end, apparently, I needn't have bothered.

"Some lady detective came by the bowling alley today, asking me about that knife too," he said. "What does that old knife have to do with..." His question trailed off as the answer suddenly dawned on him. "Hank was killed by one of those knives?"

"Looks that way." I leaned forward on the couch. "What did you tell her?"

Al's cheeks flushed at the question as his shoulders hunched up around his ears in obvious embarrassment. "Look, Tom, I..."

"Tell me you still have it."

His face grew even redder. "I'm sorry..."

My heart leapt into my throat. I wanted to scream at him. Tell him to "please still have the knife, please!"

"I lost it a few years back," he finally said. "When Cindy and I moved into this place. I dunno, it just never made the move with us. I figured I must have lost it among all the boxes and such.

I never had the heart to tell you because I know how proud of them you were."

My heart sank. He could have been telling the truth. I hoped to the Lord above he was telling the truth. But there was no way to prove it. No way to know for sure. My shoulders sagged as I leaned back into the couch cushions.

"I'm really sorry, Tom. You've got no idea how—"

"Look, I'm not upset over your losing the knife," I told him. "That's not the issue. But the fact that you don't have it anymore just sent you to the top of those detectives' suspect list. That's what I'm upset about."

Al blinked at this. After a moment, his eyes widened in understanding. "Oh."

"Yeah. 'Oh' is right. This just got a lot more complicated." I took another sip of eggnog, then decided to change strategies. "So, look. We need to establish your alibi now, I guess. If you have an alibi, then they can't touch you, right?"

Al stared up at the ceiling in thought, slowly nodding. "Yeah. Yeah, I guess."

"So, where were you two nights ago and into the morning?"

"Easy. I was at the alley," he said. "We had a special kids' night with a visit from Santa Claus. Had about forty or fifty kids. With their parents. Lots of people saw me."

I was relieved to some degree, but not completely. Although I figured Al had played Santa for the event, in full costume, I could see Detective Tice claiming it would be hard to truly place him there. Of course, it wouldn't be hard to argue that someone of his overwhelming size and boisterous personality could be hard to miss.

"What time was the event over?" I asked.

"We stayed open till ten that night. My manager, Drew, and the girl who runs the concession stand all closed with me. Probably got out of there around eleven."

I had no idea exactly when Hank had been killed, but I knew from what Jose had told me that he had left the bar some time after midnight. The bowling alley wouldn't be a good alibi after all.

"And after that?"

"Went straight home. Kids were already in bed. Cindy's the only one who saw me after that."

A doting wife who couldn't be coerced to testify against her husband would hardly be deemed a trustworthy witness—especially for someone who didn't know the Garcias like I did.

I let out a defeated sigh and shook my head. "This is a problem, Al. If I were you, I'd do whatever I could to find that knife. It might be your only option once the cops start looking at other possibilities."

His eyebrows creased with worry, and he bit down on his lower lip, then he nodded. "Kids' last day of school before the Christmas break is tomorrow. Cindy and I will tear the place apart while they're gone. If it's here, we'll find it."

I smiled. "Good. I hope you do." Then a new thought hit me. "Hey. Of all of us, you probably knew Hank the best."

"Before he took to drinking, yeah," he said grimly. "But you know my history. I couldn't be around someone like that. Couldn't risk relapsing. Not after all the crap I had to go through to get sober."

I remembered the sobriety chip I'd found yesterday while searching for clues. Just another thing that didn't bode well for my old friend's innocence. I pushed the thought aside and continued.

"And no one has ever blamed you for it. But I'm curious. Can you think of anyone who'd want to kill Hank? I mean really kill him? I know lots of people have been angry with him over the years, but I can't think of a single person who'd actually want to see him dead."

Al laughed at this before shifting in his seat and placing his empty mug down on the end table next to his recliner. "Then you don't know your friends as well as you think you do, Tom. You want a suspect to look into? Why not take a long, hard look at your pal George?"

I opened my mouth to respond, then closed it just as quickly. The accusation had taken me aback, and I wasn't entirely sure what to say. There had been bad blood between Alphonso and George Trabor for many years. Accusations about George being a bigot—especially against people in the Hispanic community in Florida—and about how Al suspected George of persuading stores and other venues to not hire the Cuban Santa Claus for that reason. But I've known George since Horatio Longpepper took me in. I'd never once heard him say anything remotely racist or bigoted, especially about Al. In fact, most of the time, George praised the giant Cuban's love of children and his Christmas spirit.

But this particular accusation seemed beyond their petty differences. Beyond personal.

"Why...why do you say that, Al? Why would you think George would have anything to do with Hank's death?"

"You heard about the deal he made with Hank, right? The bad investor. He lost his shirt on that."

"So did Teddy Gorshon, from what I hear. Why point at George over Teddy?"

"Well, for starters, I've been spending a lot of time with Teddy lately. I'm his AA sponsor." Al let out a deep sigh. He obviously didn't feel comfortable discussing any of this, but I had a feeling he was willing to do so for Trixie's benefit. "We've talked a lot about what happened. About how his chances of getting custody of his kids went out the window with that deal, and how devastated he is because of it."

"Seems like a pretty good motive for murder to me." I couldn't believe the words had come out of my mouth. Using Teddy's name, whether directly or indirectly, so casually in a sentence about being a murderer didn't seem natural.

"Actually, it's quite the opposite," Al said. "I've talked to Teddy since hearing about Hank. He made it clear he'd never do something like that. Everything that man has done in recent months has been with one goal in mind—reconciling with his kids and having them back in his life. Going to prison for murder wouldn't be a very good approach to see that happen, now, would it?"

I took a breath and held it for a moment while I shook my head. Honestly, it wouldn't. Then again, people do irrational things all the time in the heat of the moment. But for now, I decided to give the Teddy Gorshon approach a rest.

"Okay. So maybe Teddy didn't kill him," I said. "But why would George? He's a pillar of the community. Helps a lot of people, not just at Christmas time. Seems as though he's got even more to lose than Teddy."

"Yeah," said Al. "But of all five of us, he's the only one who's actually murdered someone before."

It seemed as though the floor dropped out from under me at that bit of information. The room began to spin around me in a whirling miasma of questions, conflicting emotions, and doubt.

"I'm...I'm sorry. What?"

"It's true." There was no joy in his eyes as he said the words. No indication of malice. No vindication over perceived past wrongs. The big man hated to tell me this, I knew. "What's more, Tom...he killed the guy with a knife."

10

I forced my whirling thoughts of George Trabor out of my head as I pulled into Teddy Gorshon's driveway. Teddy's place was a small patch of near-barren land in the middle of nowhere, where the grass grew in sporadic patches, and the air—even on a cold evening like today—was filled with thousands of buzzing gnats. Woods surrounded the property, cutting Teddy's vintage silver Gulf Stream trailer off from the rest of civilization.

As I brought my car to a stop, I could see Teddy a few yards away chopping wood against the backlight of a campfire and hurling the chunks onto a large pile behind him. His face twisted into a snarl every time he brought his axe down on a log. He paused, looked over at me, and gave me a curt wave when he noticed me climbing out of the car and striding over to him.

"Tom," he said, before returning to his laborious task.

I sidled up to him, letting him split a few more logs, before clearing my throat. "Did I catch you at a bad time?"

He split another log with a fierce grunt. "Gotta get the timber ready for the big bonfire later tonight," he said. "People'll be arrivin' around eight, and I got to get everything set up before then."

I watched him for a moment, letting him work in silence. Teddy was an odd choice for a department-store Santa. Like me, he was tall and skinny. Unlike me, he did try to grow his beard out, but, much like his lawn, it was scraggly and patchy at best, with only a handful of gray hairs here and there for good measure. When on Santa duty, he was forced to wear padding under his suit, and he tried to cover his beard with theatrical hair coloring. He wasn't the best Santa I knew, but he had a passion for it, and that was worth more to me than the best portrayal of the Fat Man with no heart for it.

As for the bonfire, it was a daily tradition around this time of year for all the tourists in the area. While, normally, we didn't get snow in Florida, Teddy had a wagon custom-built to look like the classic Santa sleigh, and offered hayrides in it that culminated in a festive bonfire complete with s'mores, Christmas carols, and a visit from St. Nick for the kiddies.

I glanced at my pocket watch. Five fifteen. He still had a little under two hours. More than enough time for the uncomfortable chat I intended to have with him.

"So, I take it you heard about Hank Cobb," I said the moment he stopped for a breather. I intentionally decided to keep Alphonso out of this discussion in case it would affect their sponsor/sponsee relationship.

He eyed me under the bill of his John Deere baseball cap, then grabbed the bottle of water he'd laid on an upturned log and took a long swig.

"I heard. Couldn't have happened to a better fella."

"You don't look too happy about it."

He wheeled around on me, his eyes blazing with anger. Then he closed them and took a long, deep breath. When he opened them again, he appeared calmer.

"I should be ecstatic after what that creep did to me, but I'm not." He sighed. "Can't ever have any satisfaction now that he's gone. Can't ever get paid back."

"You mean, about the money he conned from you and George."

One of his eyebrows raised up. "You know about that?"

I nodded.

"Look, I'm really sorry. George and me...we weren't tryin' to horn in on your business or nothin'. We just wanted to start a business around something we both loved so much, and..."

I raised a hand, waving it away.

"Don't worry about it, Teddy," I told him. "Like I explained to George, I'm not upset at all. I think it would have been wonderful for you two to get into the business full-time—not just at Christmas." I paused and tilted my head. "As a matter of fact, if I'm hurt, it's only because you guys didn't come to me with your idea. I could have helped you out with it."

It was no secret to anyone that I didn't make anything remotely considered a living with Wonderland. Most of the profits, in fact, went to pay Trixie's salary, as well as her tuition. It was one of the perks of being next in line to become the vessel for the Spirit of Christmas. Money was never an issue for me.

"George told me you lost pretty much everything," I said, placing my hand gently on his shoulder.

"Every single dime." The words came out like a growl. "Money I was setting aside for Cassie's wedding when she's of age. Money I planned to use to help Theo go to school. All gone."

As Al had pointed out earlier, Teddy's most admirable trait was his love for his children, Cassie and Theo. While he and his wife had divorced two years earlier, there'd never been a day he hadn't spent with his kids. Hadn't been a day he'd failed to be their dad. As a matter of fact, after Theresa divorced him, he'd completely given up drinking—the thing that had caused the divorce to begin with—so that he could earn his children's love and respect back and feel like he deserved to be part of their lives. Everything he did, he did for their benefit, and I wished to God above that there were more fathers like him in the world.

It was one of many reasons I hoped beyond hope that he hadn't killed Hank Cobb. Despite this, I knew I had to probe, no matter how painful it might be for both of us to do so. Despite Al's assertion that George was the most likely suspect, to me it seemed as though Teddy had the best motive for wanting him dead.

"Teddy, I hate to ask this..."

"You want to know if I killed him."

I nodded. "For Trixie. If it wasn't for her, I wouldn't even think of—"

"I get it." He hefted another log onto the stump and, with one whack, split it in two. "And I don't blame you one bit." He took off his hat and wiped the sweat from his forehead with his shirt sleeve. "But no. And that's what's got me all hot and bothered right now. I wanted to. The good Lord knows I would have if it hadn't been for the kids. But someone else beat me to it, so I'll never know if my love for my kids was greater than my hatred for that S.O.B."

I stared at him, and he laughed. "My answer surprise you, Tom?"

"A little bit. Just never pictured you to be a violent man. You've always been so even-keeled. So jovial."

That made him laugh even harder this time. "You and I never really spent much time together in my drinkin' days. Sure, I played Santa even back then, but I never felt comfortable hangin' out with you and Horatio during those times. I didn't feel like I deserved it. But you'd be singing a different tune if we had spent time together. It's why I can't fault Theresa for kicking me out on my rear and divorcing me. I deserved it. I was a mean drunk back then, let me tell you."

I'd heard the stories, but the only times during his drinking days I'd seen Teddy was when he played Santa. And he'd always been fabulous at that. To my knowledge, I'd never seen him drunk in costume. It's why I'd included him among those who received the pocketknife all those years ago. I knew he was dealing with the demon of the bottle, but his ability to overcome it for the sake of the kids always seemed to make him the most courageous of us all.

"Can I ask where you were the night Hank was killed?"

He looked up at the sky, taking in the crisp cool air, and thought about it. "When was that, exactly?"

"Two nights ago, I'd say sometime between two and eight in the morning."

He looked at me, one eyebrow raised as if I was the dimmest bulb in the pack. "Now, where the heck do you think I was then? I was at home in bed." He cocked his head to the camper. "Well, at least until about 5:30 or so. Had chores to do around the property. Didn't head to town until after noon some time."

There was no point in asking whether anyone could verify it. Other than the few tourists at his Christmas bonfires, Teddy never had visitors to his place, not even his kids. Theresa wouldn't allow it. What little time he spent with them, he had to do it at her house.

I sighed, dreading my next question. "Teddy, let me ask you one more question."

"Shoot."

"Remember that custom knife I gave you a few years back?"

He smiled at this and reached into his jeans pocket. "You mean this?"

He held the knife up for me to see. The enamel Christmas

tree I'd inserted shined in the waning sunlight, which seemed to reflect the sense of relief that flooded my veins.

"I use it every day. Best Christmas present I ever got."

I smiled at this. "Just curious if you still had it."

We stood there for several moments in awkward silence. The sound of a car engine drew my attention to the dirt road off Teddy's property, and I watched for a minute as an old white pickup truck idled past, kicking up a plume of dust. I stared at the vehicle for a moment. It was so rare to see traffic out here, and this guy was moving exceptionally slow. Like he was looking for something.

The sound of Teddy clearing his throat brought me back to the here-and-now. "So, the cops are really thinking our little Trixie had something to do with killing her old man?" he asked before taking another drink from his water bottle.

"Looks that way. But they seem to be shifting their focus somewhere else, so I'm not sure what's going to happen."

"Oh, really? Who else they looking at?"

I smiled at him and thumbed my chest, which elicited a raucous bit of laughter from the thin man. "You?" He laughed some more. "I tell you, those city cops are about as sharp as a rubber mallet, ain't they? Anyone who knows you for half a second knows you ain't got a violent bone in your whole body. Sounds to me like they're just grasping at straws."

"I just hope in the end mine doesn't happen to be the shortest one," I said, as I turned and headed for my car.

"Hey, Tom?"

I turned to look at him.

"Maybe those cops should be taking a look at Vinnie Tarturo. Cobb was tangled up real good with his crew for a while. If he conned me and George, maybe he did something to Tarturo that might deserve payback or something."

I nodded my thanks and waved good-bye, climbed into the T-Bird, and drove off, just as confused by the whole mess as when I'd first arrived.

11

It was late by the time I pulled into Wonderland's parking lot. The store was now closed, and the lights were dark on the first floor. The only car in the parking lot besides mine was a cobalt-blue Chevy Camaro—one of those retro jobs that looked like they did back in the '60s with two white racing stripes over the hood—taking up two spaces near the front of the House.

Upon seeing it, I growled under my breath and made my way inside without bothering to turn on any lights, then flitted up to the second floor. My footsteps barely made a sound against the old winding staircase as I ascended, and I was happy for that small favor. I was pretty sure the House was on my side for what I was about to do, and I couldn't help the smile that crept up one side of my face.

"I wouldn't go into the parlor if I were you," the high-pitched British voice said from somewhere on the first landing. "It's nothing you're going to want to see."

The elf's admonition was little more than an invitation for me to do just that. He was egging me on, hoping I'd lose my cool and make a fool of myself.

"I already know what I'll find."

I kept ascending, not caring if I passed through Peppermint or not. The little creep should know to get out of my way by now, considering that I couldn't see him at all in the gloom. When I made it to the second floor, I hung a left around the railing and stalked toward the closed parlor door. I was just about to turn the doorknob when I heard voices inside.

"Knock it off, Seth," Trixie said from the other side of the door. "I'm serious."

"Come on, Trix," Seth Timmons protested. "I'm just trying to comfort you. That's all."

"Well, I don't need to be comforted that way. I just want you to listen, so knock it off."

There were a few inaudible hushed words between them, and I held my breath trying to listen through the old oak door. I knew it was a bit stalkerish of me, but as I've stated a number of times, Trixie was like a daughter to me, and Seth was far from my favorite person for a potential suitor.

An idea forming in my head, I smiled and backed away from the door.

"Pep, you still here?"

"Where else am I going to go? My only regret is that I didn't have time to make popcorn."

I knelt, motioning for the invisible scoundrel to come closer. "I'm about to give you something better than popcorn and a show. I'm giving you permission to *be* the show."

There was a gasp of excitement.

"Really?"

I nodded.

"But Trixie won't like it."

"When has that ever stopped you?"

I could practically hear Peppermint smirk at that. "Fine. I'll do it."

I stood, then a last-second thought crossed my mind. Pep liked Seth even less than I did, so there's no telling what antics he might play on the poor boy. "Nothing too rough, elf. Just mischief. That's all."

A sigh. "You do know how to take the fun out of everything."

I would've responded, but I knew he had already gone. Once permission to have a little fun was given, Pep wasn't about to stick around long, in case I changed my mind.

Stifling a chuckle of anticipation, I crept back to the door and pressed my ear against it. The two were still talking in low tones. They no longer seemed to be arguing, but Seth was like any other boy. One-track-minded. It wouldn't take long...

"Seth! I said stop it!"

"I'm just sitting here. I didn't do anything."

It had already begun.

"Don't give me that. You just unhooked my bra from outside my shirt."

I kind of straightened at that. My face flushed red with a mixture of embarrassment and irritation. It wasn't what I'd had in mind when I told Peppermint to make a little mischief. I didn't want him messing with Trixie, just Seth.

"Ow!" Seth shouted. "You didn't have to hit me!"

Okay, now it was getting good. I'd tried to suppress the urge to peek through the old skeleton keyhole to watch them, but my curiosity was getting the better of me. I leaned in and peered through the oblong hole cut into the door.

The two were seated on a Louis XIV love seat. Seth, a beer in hand, leaned against the highly ornate back of the couch with Trix, her feet propped up on the far armrest, leaning against him. He had his free hand draped around her waist, and he worked at stroking that side of her body with nimble fingers.

"What are you talking about?" she asked him. "How could I hit you? My arms are in front of me."

"I just felt a hand slap the back of my head."

Trixie stared up at the high ceiling for a second, then looked toward the door and scowled.

Uh-oh.

She sat up, glancing around the room with furrowed brows.

"Okay, Pep," I whispered from behind the door. "Time to knock it off. She's on to us."

If the elf heard my warning, I guess he decided to ignore me. The next thing I saw was the beer bottle in Seth Timmons's hand slipping and falling into his lap, soaking it. With a cry, he jumped up from his seat, patting away the liquid from his jeans.

Trixie spun around to look at him. "What happened?"

The kid cursed, still wiping at his crotch. "Bottle slipped out of my hand," he said. "No big deal."

She peered at the door with murder in her eyes. "Oh, it's a big deal, all right," she said. "You've got no idea how big a deal it is."

Thinking she was directing her ire at him for spilling the stuff over the antique—and quite expensive, I might add—love seat, he gestured wildly at the upholstery. "I'm so sorry, Trix. I'll have it cleaned. I promise. I don't know what happened. It was like the bottle just shot out from my fingers."

"It's not your fault." She patted him on the shoulder, then stood on her tiptoes and gave him a peck on the cheek. "But I think you should probably go. I need to have a chat with my over-protective boss, and then I need to turn in and get some sleep."

His brows arched hopefully. "Want some company?"

She rolled her eyes and pointed toward the door I was standing behind. "I'll see you tomorrow, Seth. Have a good night."

With that, she turned and strode toward the door at the opposite end of the room and walked out. I watched as Seth started coming my way, realizing the embarrassment I was about to feel if I didn't scram out of there fast. I stood up and speed-walked away, rounding the corner, and nearly bumped into a very angry Trixie McNamara—her arms crossed over her chest.

I offered her a sheepish shrug, and she held up one ebony-painted fingertip to her lips to keep me quiet. Her right eyebrow was raised, letting me know just how miffed at me she was. A moment later, we heard the door to the parlor open, and Seth's heavy footsteps followed soon after, finally descending the staircase. We both held our breaths, waiting for the telltale sound of the front door. When she was certain the boy was gone, she unleashed all her fury at me.

"What's the big idea?" she shouted. "Sending Pep in there to mess with us! How could you do that to me? I thought we…"

She kept going like that, not letting me get a word in, and dressing me down as if I were an eight-year-old kid who'd just gotten caught peeking at his presents before Christmas morning. I was pretty sure my cheeks flushed with every color in the rainbow from the verbal shellacking she was giving me. But she didn't relent. I knew her well enough to know that my best course of action was simply to let her vent until she had no more air to blow. Trix had a temper, but she was quick to forgive once the fireworks had stopped.

"…seriously, the most immature idiot I've ever known," she continued. "You're supposed to be the grown-up in this relationship…"

I glanced around the hallway, wondering if Peppermint was hiding out, enjoying the show. He'd probably set me up to get this reaction from her to begin with. I'd wanted him to be a bit more subtle with his trickery toward Seth. Instead, he'd gone full-blown poltergeist on them. I could imagine him now giggling away at my discomfort, and I promised myself I'd get payback.

The sudden silence ripped me from my thoughts. I looked up to see Trixie glaring at me, arms still crossed, and one foot tapping on the hardwood floor of the hallway.

"Well?" she asked.

I suddenly felt like I should have been paying more attention to her rant. I was caught in her crosshairs and wasn't sure how to respond.

"'Well,' what?"

"That's all you have to say?"

"No. No." I shook my head emphatically, deciding to answer with the first thing that popped into my head. "How about some ice cream?"

We stood there for an uncomfortable moment, her eyes burning a hole right through me. I grinned. She tried to hold on to her anger, but I could see I'd already disarmed her. She burst out laughing, then nodded.

"Sure. Ice cream sounds pretty good right about now."

The two of us sat at the kitchen table, sharing a single bowl of ice cream drenched in hot fudge, bananas, and a couple of cherries. We didn't talk for a long time as we savored the delicious frozen treat and each other's company.

For the first time that day, I took a good long look at her. Though I'd known her her whole life and would therefore always think of her as that sweet pigtailed girl I remembered, she'd never looked more like a woman than at that moment. She'd matured so much over the last few years. Although she still insisted on dressing like a teenage Morticia Addams, with black skirts, black thigh-high stockings, dark lipstick, and choker necklaces, her spirit and personality were nearly the polar opposite. Gone was the morose, fatalistic, bordering-on-depression cynic who had attempted to steal money from my cash register. The woman before me now had been happy—until the death of her father, anyway. She was caring, sensitive, and strong. Quick to laugh, and easy to offer a smile. I couldn't have been prouder of who she had become, and I knew without a doubt that I would do whatever it took to prove that she'd had nothing to do with Hank Cobb's murder.

"So, how's the investigation going?" she asked, as if reading my mind. She plopped her spoon on the table in front of her and leaned back with an ice-cream glow.

"Slow," I told her. "Speaking of, do you remember the knife I gave Hanky when you were about five years old? The Swiss Army one with the Christmas tree on it?"

She nodded. "I remember it. Hanky yelled at me once when he found me playing with it." She paused. "That was before Mom left. When he was still a decent dad. Why do you ask?"

"I'm trying to account for them all. Was wondering if you knew if Hank still had it or not."

"No idea. He loved that thing, though. Can't imagine him ever getting rid of it." Trixie paused. "Unless he ended up pawning it off for booze money."

"Just figured I'd ask. I knew it was a long shot."

"He was killed with one of those knives, wasn't he?"

I hesitated to answer her. How much is too much information when you're talking to a girl about her father's murder? In the end, I knew she'd be angry with me if I didn't tell her the truth.

"That's the working theory, yeah."

"So, that means whoever killed Hanky was one of the Santa gang." She stewed on that a moment before shaking her head. "No. Uh-uh. I don't buy it. None of them are capable of anything like that. You need to find better suspects or something."

"Suspects aren't an issue," I told her. "Seems like we've got suspects running out the wazoo, but no real leads."

She tilted her head in thought. "Can't you...ya know...do the Santa thing to figure it out?"

I smiled. "Santa thing?"

"You know. 'He knows if you are sleeping. He knows when you're awake. He knows when you've been bad or good.' The Santa thing."

This time I laughed. It was only yesterday that I'd considered the same exact thing. "It doesn't really work like that. First of all, I'm not Santa yet. Second, I'm not even sure it works that way for the Krin'Ghal. The Spirit of Christmas isn't a spy that peers in through your window at night. It's more like an ephemeral sense of peace that washes over people. An unbridled joy that changes us from within. The good and bad thing, it's a matter of the heart. A matter of the spirit. Those who have it suddenly have a desire to do what's right. To love their neighbors. It's not a threat to the wicked, but a promise to the wise."

Her eyes rolled sarcastically behind her dark eyeliner. "So, that's a *no*."

"That'd be a *no*. Correct. Unfortunately, if we're going to solve the murder, I'm going to have to do it the old-fashioned way."

"Like Sherlock Holmes."

I took one more mouthful of ice cream, then pushed away from the table feeling as though my shirt was about to pop open.

"I wish. But I'll do my best anyway." I got up from the table, picking up the ice-cream bowl and spoons and carrying them over to the sink. "So, how you holding up, kiddo?"

"Okay, I guess." She leaned back in her chair and stared up at the ceiling. "It's just all so surreal right now. I can't believe he's gone. Can't believe they think I killed him."

I turned on the tap and rinsed the ice cream off of the dinnerware. "I don't think it's so much they suspect you, as it is they've got no one else to point a finger at right now. You were the easiest target." I thought about the conversation I'd had with Tice earlier that day. "Sooner or later, they'll turn their attention to other possible suspects."

"Like you?" I could hear her swallow hard, as if the words were catching in her throat. "I won't let them pin this on you. Even if I have to confess to the murder myself, I won't let them accuse you of killing Hank."

I froze for a moment, contemplating the meaning of what she had just said, then set the now-clean bowl in the dish rack and turned to look at her.

"Pep told me about your talk with that detective," Trixie answered my unspoken question. "Told me the House didn't like the way he was talking to you either."

I smiled. "Nothing to worry about. If the police won't bother to find the real murderer, we'll just have to do their job for them."

"Still, this kind of thing isn't supposed to happen," she told me. "You're the best thing that ever happened in my life. You're more of a father to me than that man ever was. Plus, you're going to be Santa Claus one day, man. The *real* freaking Santa Claus. Santa Claus isn't ever supposed to be a murder suspect."

I beamed at her. Although she'd grown up so much in recent years, in many ways she was still just a little girl who wore overly dramatic makeup and macabre clothing. "And a house isn't supposed to have a thirteen-foot alligator living in its walls," I said, gesturing around the room. "But here we are. Things happen whether we want them to or not. We'll get through it." I walked over to her, leaned down, and kissed her on her forehead. "Now, I'm going to bed. Feel free to stay here tonight if you want. I think you'll probably feel better in the morning."

She smiled up at me. Her ebony mascara was once again streaking her face. We hugged each other for several moments; then both of us retired to our respective rooms for a much-needed night of rest.

12

Try as I might, I couldn't sleep. Lying deep in my sleigh bed, I tossed and turned, but the events of the last two days kept replaying over and over in my head like a series of old reruns. I kept seeing the dead man in the grimy old Santa suit lying face down on my showroom floor, a very familiar knife beside him. Kept seeing the two police detectives' suspicious eyes staring me down. Trixie's makeup-streaked face, Trix herself being led away in handcuffs.

And the stories I'd been told by my suspects—the worst of which included the accusation that one of my oldest friends, George Trabor, had stabbed a man to death.

Despite the double layer of blankets and comforters and the fireplace on the other side of my bedroom, I shivered. My room was growing increasingly chilly, and I now worried about the strange snowfall the House, as well as the town of Christmas, had experienced yesterday. I knew Peppermint was right, even though I was loath to admit it. It was the churning emotional tumult welling up within me that was the cause of it all, and there was nothing I knew that could stop it.

I rolled over once more, my eyes drifting to the set of bay windows on the north side of my turret apartment. The silver rays of the moon cast shadows across my floor, and I considered trying to reach out to Krin'Ghal for help. But I knew that would be useless. The Spirit of Christmas was dormant now, awaiting the moment—now less than a week away—that it would awaken and spread its cheer around the world in the guise of Santa Claus.

It's not that Krin'Ghal isn't real, per se. Santa, especially within its human vessel, is real enough. Powerful. Very wise. And full of the most awe-filled sense of peace you can ever imagine. But it also has its place. Its purpose. And it can't really go beyond what it was put on Earth to do. No, the truth is that, in situations like this, it could only point me to something...someone...even more powerful and wise.

I closed my eyes and said my silent prayer. I wasn't sure it would help, but I also knew there was little else I could do at that moment.

CRASH!

My eyes snapped open at the sound from downstairs. My heart suddenly pounded against my chest.

Was that glass breaking?

I lay perfectly still, holding my breath, and listening. Seven, eight, nine heartbeats later, I sucked in a lungful of air and held it again.

Nothing. No other sounds.

My heart rate slowed. It had probably been a trick of the wind, or the old House shifting in its own slumber.

Then the sound of cursing from downstairs. Deep-throated growls of frustration, followed by a series of shrieking screams. It didn't take much to imagine what was happening. Someone had just broken in and was now facing untold horrors hurled at them by the House. The more severe the obstacle, the more the shouts escalated.

I rolled my eyes with an irritated sigh. I almost pitied whoever was downstairs. Breaking into this place was never wise—which made me wonder once again about the sort of person who'd managed to get inside to kill Hank Cobb.

"Are you going to go down there and see what's going on?" Peppermint's crisp English accent carried far more disdain than normal. I guess he was still miffed about how Trixie and I had made up so splendidly after his antics in the parlor earlier. "Sounds like someone isn't having much of a pleasant burglary."

I groaned, still nice and cozy in my blankets. "Ugh. Do I have to?"

The elf sniffed with contempt, egging me on as the master of the House to do what needed doing. I sighed and sat up in my bed, casting aside the thick mound of bedding, and shivered. It was far colder in the house than I'd realized, and I could barely feel any heat emanating from the fireplace. I pulled my robe over my silk crimson PJs, grabbed a baseball bat I kept in an umbrella stand by my door, and crept out of my room.

"Obviously you already know what's going on downstairs," I whispered as we sneaked toward the third-story staircase. "Mind giving me a heads-up?"

There was no response from the elf, which meant either that he'd already left me to fend for myself or he was simply ignoring me to ramp up the anxiety congealing in my limbs. I tightened my grip on the bat and tiptoed down the stairs, my ears straining to listen for more sounds below.

I heard nothing else until I'd rounded the second-floor landing and could peer past the railing into the showroom. A few of the Christmas lights still blinked on and off around the trees, giving off a sort of strobe effect of the surroundings. I watched as two shadows skulked around the main Christmas tree, scrambling on hands and knees as if they were searching for something.

"I'm tellin' ya, Jimmy, somethin' grabbed my leg," one of the shadows hissed to the other. "That's why I fell t'ru da window like dat."

"Maybe so, but didja have to scream like a lil girl?"

Somewhat amused by the exchange, I set the bat down along one of the steps and leaned against the banister, resting my chin on my forearms to watch.

"Somethin' grabs yer legs in a creepy ol' house you're breakin' into and see if youse don't scream too."

The two spoke with thick Brooklyn accents and were large brutes, from their shapes. But I could already tell they weren't exactly rocket scientists.

"That was me," Peppermint suddenly whispered while trying to suppress a giggle. "I'm the one that grabbed the bloke's leg. You should have seen the look on his face."

I jumped at the sudden intrusion. "Geez. I need to hang a bell around your neck or something."

"Wouldn't work." There was a pause. "Now, about our bur-glars...you just going to let them pilfer your wares, or what?"

There was little to be worried about for the moment. Between the House and Peppermint, they wouldn't be allowed to steal anything of value. So I was inclined to remain hidden within the shadows of the staircase and watch the exchange further. I was intrigued as to what they were looking for. They didn't seem at all interested in any of the merchandise, and instead busied themselves peering under furniture and rifling through drawers.

I shrugged. "Right now, I'm more interested in what they're after." My eyes zoomed back and forth, watching them as if I were in the bleachers at Wimbledon. "Besides, I'm sure the House already has things under control."

"I wouldn't count on that," the elf replied. "She's been acting rather peculiar since the murder, I think."

"Well, we'll just play it by ear. Be ready. If necessary, I'll need you to do your thing."

I could almost hear the little imp salivate at that. "Just what I wanted to hear." Apparently, he'd already forgotten about how his shenanigans from earlier hadn't worked to drive an insurmountable wedge between Trix and me.

"So, what are we lookin' for again, Jimmy?" the first goon asked his partner.

"How should I know? Cobb probably put it in a duffel bag or somethin'," Jimmy said. "Now keep yer trap shut, Louis, and keep lookin'."

"But we've looked everywhere. It's not here. What if that Christmas guy's already found it, and is hiding it upstairs or somethin'?"

Jimmy straightened up at the suggestion, scratching his head under his wool cap. "Dat's a good point, Louis. Boss didn't say nothin' about where we should be lookin'. But dis is a big ol' house—three stories from what I could tell from outside—it might be upstairs for all we know."

The smarter of the two burglars turned toward the staircase and drew what looked like a revolver from the back of his pants.

The floorboards of the House rumbled.

"Uh-oh," Peppermint said. "She doesn't much care for goons with guns, does she?"

I shook my head. "It appears she does not."

Louis drew his own weapon, a much larger handgun than the snub-nose of his partner.

A deep groan rumbled from the walls now.

The two burglars stopped in their tracks and glanced furtively around.

"Did you hear that?" Louis asked his partner.

"That growlin' sound?" Jimmy answered.

Louis nodded, then gulped.

"Nope. Didn't hear a thing." He waved for his friend to follow, and they both carefully crept toward the staircase.

As they drew nearer, I could tell these men weren't built for the stealth necessary for a successful burglary career. Armed robbery, maybe. But not second-story jobs requiring finesse and grace. If they happened to run into me—or, worse, Trixie—while in the commission of their crime, I had no doubt they'd shoot first, and feel bad about it later. Maybe.

"Are you sure about this?" Louis, who was still several feet behind his partner, asked.

"Boss wants what Cobb stole from him," Jimmy spat back. "We get boss what he wants. No matter what."

Okay, so that's interesting. Hank Cobb apparently stole something of great value to someone. And considering these two Mensa members' brogues, I'm willing to bet I know who that someone is.

Of course, that knowledge didn't make me feel any better. Christmas's own semi-retired gangster, Vinnie Tarturo, wasn't exactly someone you wanted to deal with while trying to beat a murder charge.

They were within three feet of the staircase now, and I froze. At that moment, I was cloaked in enough shadow that they'd only see me by looking directly at me. But that wouldn't last long. If I moved, they'd spot me. If I didn't, they'd walk right up the stairs until they were next to me. I was out of options.

"Pep," I whispered.

"Yes, boss?"

I was just about to unleash the house elf on the two intrud-ers, when another growl rumbled from somewhere downstairs. But it wasn't the House making the noise this time.

"Did you hear that?" Louis asked, whirling around with his gun shaking in his hand.

The growl came again, tumbling in on itself like sticks on a kettle drum.

"...the heck is that?" Jimmy spat, bringing his own revolver around in search of the source of the noise.

Something struck a display stand, and it tumbled over to their left. The two criminals spun in that direction with a shout.

"I saw something!" Louis barked. "It was big!"

"What? What did you see?"

Louis, the larger of the two, sucked in lungfuls of air as his eyes swept the floor. His gun hand continued to shake.

"I'd rather not say."

"Come on, man. Tell me!"

Their voices were louder now. They no longer seemed to care if anyone upstairs heard them.

Something thudded along the wooden floors behind them— the sound of something heavy moving fast. They turned toward the sound, scanned the room, and both gasped at the same time.

I knew what they'd seen, and my pulse quickened. The two men were in far more danger than I would have liked. Consider-ing that there had already been one murder in the store this week, I'd hate to have to report two more bodies before the weekend. Steeling myself, I drew in a breath, crouched down behind the banister, and prepared to speak.

"Gentlemen!" I shouted.

The two men turned their gun barrels in the direction of my voice. Unable to identify my exact location, they held their fire, thankfully.

"I must warn you, you both are in grave danger," I continued. "It appears that our watch dog has been released, and he is stalking you."

"That wasn't no dog!" shouted Louis.

"Indeed, it wasn't," I responded. "In fact, it was an alligator. Thirteen feet long, to be precise. And not very fond of unwelcome guests."

Jimmy laughed nervously. "An alligator? Yeah, right."

"You just saw him, didn't you?" I asked. "Or at least his shadow. I can assure you that Tinsel is very, very real. He took up residence in our House twenty-seven years ago, and we've been unable to have him removed. So we simply give him a wide berth and respect his right to live here with us. If I could call him off, I most certainly would. But he's never been one to listen to me."

The burglars still had their guns pointed in my general direction but hadn't spotted me yet. As much as Louis's hands were shaking, I feared he'd probably hit me by accident if his finger flexed at the wrong moment. I prayed his gun didn't have a hair trigger.

"Never been one to listen to you?" Peppermint laughed. "You've never even seen him. I thought you didn't believe he actually existed."

It's true. Although I liked to tease Trixie about the alligator, I'd never actually seen it. I'd been told the alligator lived in the secret passages of the mansion by Horatio when I'd first come to work for him. Peppermint had enjoyed spinning yarns about the ancient reptile, insisting that he was real. Even Trixie herself claimed to have caught a glimpse of its tail once as she explored the labyrinth of passages. But in truth I'd never once laid eyes on ol' Tinsel and wasn't sure I even believed the stories I'd been told.

"They don't know that. Now, hush."

Another growl rumbled just off to their left. They spun and fired two shots into the shadows. This time, the House itself responded, shaking with fury as the projectiles slammed into its flooring. The crystalline chandelier hanging from the domed ceiling shook, raining shards of glass and metal down on the intruders. The two men ducked, covering their heads from the debris, and darted toward the counter that supported the cash register.

Huddled behind the counter, the two men spoke in hushed whispers. From my position, I couldn't hear what they were saying, but I could tell by their movements that Louis was begging his partner to leave. I watched as Jimmy's head shook adamantly. He had no intention of going back to their boss empty-handed. Louis pointed frantically to the broken window near the front door—presumably where they'd entered the shop—but still his partner refused.

That's when I heard the ear-splitting crack of wood and watched in horror as a jagged seam split along the floor in their direction. As the seam stretched toward them, floorboards splintered, jutting up into the air like wooden fangs. The seam widened, opening up into a gaping chasm and threatening to swallow the burglars whole.

With a scream, Louis leaped over the counter to avoid falling into the pit and dashed to the window. He dove headfirst through the opening and disappeared from view. Jimmy, his eyes stretched wide at the approaching abyss, hesitated for a span of two heartbeats, then followed his partner's path and fled from the house as fast as he could.

With the two gone, the House began to settle. The rumbling subsided and the jagged tear in the floor stopped widening. The chandelier rocked back and forth for a moment or two, but soon leveled off to a gentle swing. There was no sign of any alligator to be seen, but that didn't surprise me.

I let out a sigh and tumbled back onto the step I'd been perched upon, brushing my fingers through my mop of bright orange hair. That had been a close one. I wasn't sure whether the House would have followed through with swallowing the two thugs or not, but I'd already decided that when this mess was over, she and I were going to have to sit down for a long talk about her temper.

"Um, guys?" a female voice called softly from downstairs. I scrambled to my feet and peered over the banister to see Trixie in her pajamas gawking at the jagged opening in the floor. Her hair was askew with a major case of bedhead, and she peered sleepily over the rims of her coke-bottle glasses at the mess. "What the heck happened here?"

I smiled down at her and thumbed toward the kitchen door. "Put a kettle on the stove," I told her. "I'll tell you all about it over a bit of tea after I call the police."

13

After the thugs had fled, I changed out of my pajamas and into my suit before placing two calls. The first was to the Orange County Sheriff's Office. The other was to Ursula.

By the time the police arrived, the floor had already repaired itself, the glass bobbles once more hung from the chandelier, and the broken windowpane was back in one piece. That last bit had been sort of an annoyance because I'd had to break it again to prove that a burglary had, in fact, taken place.

Sometimes the House's efficiency in tidying itself up could be more of a hindrance than a blessing.

Now I found myself back in the kitchen being grilled by detectives Tice and Lassiter. I sat in my chair, mesmerized by the bulging veins protruding from the male detective's forehead, as he bombarded me with pointed questions that I struggled to make sense of.

"For the last time, what were these burglars looking for?" Tice growled, slamming the palm of his hand down on the table.

"Why are you badgering me? I'm the *victim* here!"

Detective Lassiter placed her hand on her partner's shoulder, trying to calm him. "David," she said. "Maybe you should go out and interview the girl. Let me talk with Mr. Nast for a while, okay?"

The large cop glared at her for a moment, then his face

softened. He gave her a nod, got up, and walked out of the kitchen, leaving me alone with the much prettier detective.

"I'm sorry about that," she said with an understanding smile. "David's set to retire at the beginning of the year, and he's a bit burned out. This is his last case, so he's a little stressed over it."

"You think *he's* stressed," I told her. "How do you think I feel?"

She nodded at this without a word, then opened her notebook. "Let me rephrase what my partner was trying to ask. Do you have any notion what our suspects might have been looking for in your store?"

I pondered the question, wondering just how much I should tell her about the exchange I'd heard between the two intruders during their search. In the end, I decided the best course of action was to be as frank as possible.

"I overheard them," I said. "They said that Hank had apparently stolen something from their boss."

"Their boss?"

I shrugged. "They didn't mention him by name, but I couldn't help wondering if Vinnie Tarturo had something to do with it. They seemed like his sort of associates, and Hank had known dealings with the man."

Lassiter jotted the information down, then looked up at me. "And they didn't mention what had been stolen?"

I shook my head. "It never came up. But apparently one of them didn't know exactly what it was, because he asked his partner what they were looking for."

"What did the partner say?"

"He didn't know either. Said it was probably in a bag or something."

"That's not a lot to go on."

"If they'd said anything more, I promise I would tell you."

"Are you sure about that?" she asked, eyeing me suspiciously.

"What is that supposed to mean?"

She pursed her lips. "Well, we've been hearing about your little investigation, Mr. Nast. I know David talked to you yesterday about speaking with Jose Jimenez at Stuart's Pub. Seems like everybody we go to interview about this case tells us they've talked to you first. You've been warned about investigating this matter, and yet you seem determined to ignore that warning. It has us wondering why."

"Why do you think?" I said. "First, you all but accuse poor Trixie of murdering her own father. Then, yesterday, your partner starts insinuating that I might have had something to do with it. It's fight or flight, Detective. With your focus on us, I'm afraid the real killer just might get away with it, and either Trix or myself will get the blame. No, thank you. I'll do what I can to clear our names if that's all right with you."

Just then, the kitchen floor rumbled beneath my feet as if the House were once again inexplicably upset. I didn't think it had anything to do with the conversation with Lassiter. Then I remembered that Tice was in the other room, grilling Trixie. I stood to go to her rescue from the brutish detective.

Before I could take a step, there was a tap at the kitchen door. It swung open, and Ursula and Janet Wood marched into view. Ursula stomped over to the kitchen table, dropped her patent leather briefcase on top of it, and turned to the detective.

"I think that's enough questioning for now," she told the detective. "I need to have a chat with my client."

Lassiter looked over at me, then at the stern-faced attorney. "We're only discussing the break-in, Ms. Brooks. I hardly think it requires an attorney to be present."

Ursula held up a hand. "The way you and your partner seem to have a vendetta against Mr. Nast, I hardly think your inclusion in this investigation is in the best interest of my client," she told the detective. "I've already got a call in to your sergeant requesting the assignment of new, unbiased investigators into the burglary." She gestured toward the kitchen door. "So, if you'll be so kind. I'd like to speak with Mr. Nast now, please."

The detective stared Ursula down for several seconds, no doubt trying to figure out how to get rid of this troublesome counselor. In the end, she stood from the table and looked down at me. "Mr. Nast, we'll be in touch. Please let us know if you think of anything else. Okay?"

I stood, offering my hand to her. She shook it, and I agreed to pass on to her anything new I discovered about the case in the future. With that, she strode from the kitchen without looking back.

"Is Trixie okay out there with the mean one?" I asked Ursula, who'd already taken a seat at the table. Janet, her friend and paralegal, sat down beside her before opening the briefcase filled with a myriad of papers.

"The mean one?" Ursula asked.

"Tice. The guy is brutal. I'm concerned that he's waterboarding the girl this very moment."

My ex laughed, shaking her head. "I sent him packing before I came in here. Eli Smart was outside when we first arrived... concerned when he rode his bike by and saw the police cars. He's out there now comforting her." She riffled through the papers in her case, as if searching for something in particular. "You can be pretty boneheaded sometimes, you know that?"

"Boneheaded?"

"Don't you ever watch TV?"

"Uh, not really. I prefer to read."

She rolled her eyes. "They're playing you. Oldest trick in the book. Good cop, bad cop. You never heard of it?"

I blinked, taking a glance at the door where Detective Lassiter had just exited. "Huh? But she..."

"She sent him out of the kitchen so she could have a reasonable discussion with you, right? He'd been excessively hard on you, asking irrational questions and such? Threatening you? Intimidating you?"

I nodded.

"And she persuaded him to leave. Her voice soft. Understanding. She just wanted to get to the bottom of things, and her partner has been a little stressed lately."

"It's his last case," I told her. "He's retiring."

Ursula laughed. "Seriously, Tom. You've got to start watching television more. She was fishing for information."

"Just about the burglary."

"Really?"

I thought about it a moment, then my head cocked to the side with a thought. "Well, she did take some time to discuss my own investigation. Warned me not to get involved, basically."

"But she did it in a nice way, right?" This came from the soft-spoken, nervous voice of Janet.

I gave her a nod. Yeah, I'd definitely fallen for the oldest play in the detective playbook. I felt my cheeks flush.

"All right. I get it. I'm a moron." I leaned back in the chair, its wrought-iron seat feeling very hard and uncomfortable at the moment. "So, thanks for coming. I wasn't sure you would."

Ursula found the paper she'd been searching for and shoved it in front of me, holding out a pen.

"What's this?"

"Like I said, you're my client," she said with a smirk. "Considering our past, I figured it best to make it legal and official. Don't want you to start ghosting my legal calls like you did my personal ones."

Stifling my instinct to apologize once more, I took the pen and signed the document before sliding it back over to her.

"Okay," I said. "Now what?"

She looked over at Janet, who was opening the large case she'd brought into the kitchen to reveal a 10-key stenographer's keyboard.

"Now, you're going to tell me everything that's happened since I was last here—especially the burglary tonight."

14

After the briefing, Ursula, Janet, Trixie, Eli, and I found ourselves once more out in the showroom, in the central atrium. I was certain Peppermint was lurking around as well, though I couldn't be sure. And my eyes scanned the shadows for any signs of a stray monster alligator tail that might still be lurking as well.

One could never be too careful where guard-alligators were concerned.

"Okay," Ursula began, as she hefted her cascading mane of hair into a ponytail. "So, since the murder, are you sure you haven't found anything weird that Mr. Cobb might have dropped or hidden when he was murdered?"

I rolled my eyes. "I'm pretty sure I'd remember if I'd found some gangster's stolen goods."

"Don't be so sure," she said. I noticed Janet was already on her hands and knees, peering under furniture, displays, and anything else that might conceal something sinister. "What does a *gangster's stolen goods* look like?"

Okay, she had me there.

There was a low growl that came from the bowels of the House, but no one seemed to pay attention to it, assuming it was merely settling amid the unusually cold temperatures outside. I, for one, couldn't help wondering what had gotten the old place all aflutter again, however.

"Okay, but I haven't found anything since the murder. Nothing at all. I'm sure of it." The moment I said it, something in the back of my mind began nagging me. Something I'd forgotten. Something obvious.

"So whatever it is must still be here, then."

"Unless..." Eli broke into the conversation now. "...unless Mr. Cobb's killer took it."

I thought about that for a minute and nodded. It was a distinct possibility, assuming that Vinnie Tarturo's goons hadn't been the ones to kill him. If they had, there'd have been no point in their breaking into the House tonight.

"Well, I guess we need to get to looking for it, in case it's still here." Trixie yawned. It was well past three in the morning, and we were all tired. But I had a feeling that, out of all of us, she was approaching the point of near exhaustion. The emotional roller coaster she'd been through in the last few days would sap the energy from anyone.

"Not you, young lady," I told her. "You need to go back to your room and get some sleep. We open in about five hours, and we're approaching the home stretch of the Christmas season. I have a feeling we're going to be packed, and you need your rest."

She yawned again, started to protest, then thought better of it before waving us goodnight and disappearing through one of the secret passages to her room. I turned to my remaining three companions.

"Okay, guess we need to tear this place apart."

I'm not sure why I even bothered to say it. Janet was still searching the place top to bottom, like a human top that had been wound up way too tight. Ursula joined her, leaving me to team up with Eli. While the ladies took the southeast section of the store, Eli and I took the northwest, near the front entrance and main thoroughfare.

"Come on, Mr. Nast," Eli whispered after we'd been down on our hands and knees for the better part of ten minutes. "Why not just do some of your magic and find whatever we're looking for? I've seen you and this house do some awfully wild things."

Without looking at him, my eyes widened at his last comment. Of all the people who frequented Wonderland, Eli had probably logged more hours here than anyone else. If the House's or Peppermint's shenanigans were going to be witnessed, it would surely have been by him. But I couldn't very well admit that. Nor could I explain that things didn't work that way. Yes, the House was...sentient...to some degree. It could do some amazing things. But as Pep had pointed out to me when I'd first found Hank's body, it couldn't communicate, and it rarely took orders.

"Eli, how exactly did you get roped into this, anyway?" I asked, hoping to change the subject.

He was behind me, scrambling on hands and knees, peeking underneath every piece of furniture or display along the hardwood aisle.

"Couldn't sleep, so I decided to go for a ride. Hoping to see more snow." Eli's license had been suspended ever since his DUI, so he went everywhere on his bicycle now. "Rode past the store and saw all the police cars. I was worried there'd been another murder, so I stopped to snoop and ran into Ms. Brooks and her assistant at the door. They asked me to come in and keep Trixie company until they dealt with the cops."

I nodded at this, then resumed my search along the aisle. I figured Hank couldn't have had much time between the moment he set foot in the store and when he was killed. If he'd hidden anything, it would be along the aisle where customers could easily walk.

"But you didn't answer my question," Eli continued. "Why not just use your magic to figure all this out? I don't understand."

I stopped crawling and craned my head around to look at him. "For the hundredth time, I'm *not* Santa Claus. There's nothing special about this house except its age. I'm just a guy who runs a Christmas-and-holiday emporium. That's all."

It wasn't exactly a lie. At the moment, I really wasn't Santa. And I wasn't entirely sure what animated the House, but I didn't think it had anything to do with "magic." It's all a bit of a gray area when it comes to how to keep my secret; but, for the moment, I needed to nip this Santa talk in the bud by any means necessary.

"Look, Eli..." I took a deep breath, choosing my next words carefully. The last real debate we'd had about this topic was when his father had been on his deathbed and Eli had pleaded with me to save him. Guilt swept through me at the thought, but I knew it was irrational. There really had been nothing I could do. "I like you a lot." Okay, not a horrible way to start, I figured. "But you shouldn't be throwing that kind of talk around so loosely. People will think you're crazy or something."

His bright eyes seemed to dim a little as he let out a sigh. Well, I guess I blew it in the end. So much for letting him down easy. With nothing left to say, Eli continued with his search, veering slightly away from me and into the Santa-boots section of the store.

When he was far enough away, I felt a tug on my trouser leg.

"That kid is really starting to creep me out," Peppermint whispered near my ear.

"He's a good kid. Just lonely, I think. Hopeful. Nothing wrong with that."

"And what happens if he finds something that proves his theory about you?"

I let the question wash over my thoughts as I sidled up to a potted Peace Lily and dug into the soil with my hands.

"Well, if you don't want to deal with the nerd, then let me ask you this: Are you forgetting something?" Peppermint asked.

I stopped my digging and turned in the general direction of his voice.

"What do you mean?" My eyes darted over to the two women, who were now sifting through a metal bargain bin of tree ornaments.

"You actually *did* find something odd," Pep said. "Just after the police left with Cobb's body."

My mind raced back to that day—now a whirlwind of cluttered memories and heavy emotions—and I mentally walked myself through the events step by step until I remembered.

"The Alcoholics Anonymous token." My nose crinkled at the thought. "Kind of weird sending a couple of thugs to break into a place just for a sobriety chip, don't you think?"

"Maybe Tarturo's gone sober and is really proud of his accomplishment," he said. "Either way, it *is* something. And given your teetotaling ways, it definitely didn't belong here."

I thought about that for a second, then nodded.

"Ladies!" I stood up, then glanced over at Eli. "And gentleman." The three of them turned to stare at me. "I just remembered something."

The four of us moved over to the register counter, where I began digging in my coat pocket. "Now, where did I put it?"

During my search, I withdrew a hodgepodge of odds and ends, dropping them on the countertop. A compass, some string, a yo-yo, three sets of keys I no longer knew what they opened, a deck of vintage baseball cards featuring a Pete Rose rookie-of-the-year card, and a television remote control. The last one was odd considering, as Ursula had pointed out, that I didn't even own a TV. The collection of junk on the counter continued piling up until, finally, my fingers found what they were looking for, and I withdrew my hands with a cry of "Eureka!"

I held the sobriety chip in the air for them. In return, they each stared back at me with blank expressions.

"What's that?" Ursula finally asked.

I glanced at the token, front and back, then looked back at her. "It's an Alcoholics Anonymous chip," I told her, as if the answer should have been obvious.

"I know that. What's its significance?"

"I found it. Under that sofa." I pointed to the piece of furniture in question. "The day Hank Cobb was killed."

"Again, this area is open to the public on a daily basis. Anyone could have dropped it. What's the significance?"

I blinked. How could I explain that my House, sentient as it was, didn't abide clutter, and that if the chip had been there for any length of time more than an hour or two, it would have simply disappeared into the ether without so much as a "thank you very much." Since it was still there when I returned to the store that morning, logic dictated that it could only have been left by either the killer or Hank Cobb. Granted, having heard of Hank's recent desires to turn his life around, it might have come from him. But somehow I doubted he'd been sober long enough to earn a six-month chip.

"Um, well..." was my most articulate explanation.

"Tom, as you know, I'm in AA myself," Janet said, taking the chip from my hand to give it a closer look. "I've had a few of these over the years. Though significant to the owner for what they represent, they're basically a dime a dozen. Even if it was somehow connected to the murder, there's no way to trace it to the owner. Ya know, the whole 'anonymous' part and all." She handed the token back to me. "Sorry. I don't think it's much of a clue."

The walls surrounding us cracked and popped as if a great weight were pressing down on the House's foundations. This time, my three guests noticed, their eyes widening at the sound.

"Geez, Tom," Ursula said. "I think you need to have someone come look at the place for structural problems. This winter weather seems to be playing havoc with it."

Eli huffed. "Yeah," he said. "The *weather's* doing it."

I glared at him, wishing he'd drop this whole Santa/Magic House business once and for all. Eventually, someone significant might start paying attention.

That's when I heard the wind howling past the windows. I walked over to them and, while it was still quite dark out, I could see the telltale sight of flakes of snow whirling across the parking lot. Maybe it *was* the weather after all, and nothing to do with the House being upset.

I smiled sheepishly. "Yeah, maybe you're right." I straightened my tie, then gestured toward the window. "Either way, it's looking pretty bad out there," I told them. "Looks like we're going to get more than flurries today. You three might want to think about getting home before it gets too bad to drive out there."

"Are you sure?" Ursula asked. "We haven't found what the burglars were after yet."

"And I don't think we will. Whatever they were looking for, I don't think it's here or we would have found it already." *Or the House would have already discarded it.*

With that, the two women said their good-byes and walked out of the store. I stood on the front porch, watching them get into Ursula's Porsche and drive off.

"Mr. Nast," Eli said, reminding me that I still had one outsider left to get rid of. I tensed, ready for him to spout off another Santa theory. "That sobriety chip," he continued, surprising me. "Don't let those two discourage you about it. I think it's a great clue."

I looked over at him. He was beaming from ear to ear. "I mean, how many people on your suspect list could be in AA, right?"

I mentally calculated my suspects and was surprised to realize there were far more on the list than I had ever imagined. Teddy and Al, right off the top of my head. She wasn't a suspect, but even Janet was in AA. Heck, who else? Seemed Christmas was rife with alcohol addiction.

Instead of voicing any of this, I merely shrugged before offering the kid a quick wave. "Better get you home, Eli." I nodded to the falling snow. "I can give you a ride if you don't want to bike home."

"Nah, I'm good," he said as he clambered onto his bicycle. "I'm from Florida, born and raised. I'm going to enjoy this weather while I can."

With that, he pedaled off, out of view of the parking-lot lights.

With everyone finally gone, and after ensuring that everything was locked up tight, I motioned to the broken window. "All right, House. It's all yours."

I began making my way upstairs, looking forward to the couple of hours' sleep I would be able to get before the store opened its doors again. I had no doubt that by the time I came downstairs again, the window would be repaired, the customers would be here in droves, and I would be presented with another assortment of problems I'd have to deal with before this murder case was finally laid to rest.

15

I t hadn't snowed inside the House for the few hours of sleep
I'd managed to get. The same couldn't be said for outside,
though. When I awoke that morning and opened my curtains, I gasped at the sight of the snow accumulating on the
lawn below. There wasn't much of the white stuff, but there
was enough that it was sticking. The world beyond my window
seemed sprinkled in a thin layer of white powder as far as the eye
could see.

I blinked, making sure I wasn't hallucinating. When I decided it was, indeed, real, I turned on the radio to listen to the
news while I got ready for the day ahead.

"That was Gene Autry's 1949 classic 'Rudolph the Red-
Nosed Reindeer,'" came the DJ for WXMS 105 FM. "For those
of you just waking up and getting ready for work, you might
want to plan on leaving a few minutes early. It's crazy out there.
So far, this is the worst snowfall we've seen here in Central Florida since the storm of 1977, and meteorologists are predicting
the next few days are only going to get worse. So, wrap up warm,
drive safe, and let's look forward to an unusual white Christmas
this year!"

With that, Eartha Kitt's sultry rendition of "Santa Baby"
came over the speakers, and I hopped in the shower.

Twenty minutes later, I was downstairs. It was still nearly an
hour before opening time, so I thought I'd take a few minutes

to do some mindless labor before I dove headfirst into panicky customers with only a few more shopping days left—and my own little private investigation.

It wasn't long before Trixie came out, dressed in a black-and-burgundy ensemble, complete with leather choker. Her shoulder-length raven-hued hair was now highlighted with a few strands of red and green. She smiled at me when she saw me working.

"Good morning," she said, making her way over to the coffee machine behind the counter. "Did you guys have any luck last night after I went to bed?"

"No. Honestly have no idea what those goons were looking for." I paused, a new thought forming in my head. I wanted to smack myself for not thinking to ask it before. "Trixie?"

She turned to look at me. "Yeah?"

"Why was your dad wearing a Santa suit the other night?"

She glanced up at the ceiling, as if pondering the question for all it was worth. Then she shrugged. "I'm not really sure. He came into the bar wearing it. Told me he was trying to change, getting himself straight, and wanted me to give him another chance." She poured a cup of coffee into her "Have a Gothic Christmas" mug and continued. "Maybe he thought the Santa suit was his way of giving me a gift. My dad...getting back to his roots. Playing Santa again and all that. Maybe he thought he had to compete with you. I dunno."

She paused for a second. "Weird thing is, even though I didn't think about it at the time, it was strange seeing him sober. I can't remember the last time I'd ever seen him like that."

"Sober?" I stiffened. It jibed with everything I was learning about his final days, but I still struggled to believe it. "You mean, he wasn't drinking? At the bar?"

"Didn't act like it. He seemed more sober than I'd ever seen him in my life." She turned away from me as she took a sip of her coffee, but it wasn't quick enough to keep me from seeing her eyes glistening with repressed tears. "But then, I was too young to remember him before he started drinking."

With her back still to me, Trixie sniffed and wiped an unbidden tear from her cheek. I walked over to her, placing an arm around her shoulder and giving her a squeeze. "I'm sorry."

"For what?"

"Making you relive it all over again. Having to live with the memory of your last conversation with him being an argument." I tightened my hold on her shoulder again. "Having to deal with him your whole life as a father."

She wiped at her eyes. "At least I had a father." She smiled up at me. "You never even knew yours. I guess I'm lucky compared to what you must have gone through, growing up."

We separated, and I walked over to the coffee machine to pour a cup of brew for myself. "I don't know. Remember, in a way, I was raised by Santa Claus...every child's dream, right?"

She smiled more brightly at this. "Something I've sort of been able to experience since the day we met."

We spent the rest of the early morning preparing for the store's opening in silence. All the while, my mind kept returning to Hank and his tattered, grime-covered Santa costume. There'd been something about it that had been nudging the back of my mind for the past couple of days. Something was missing. I couldn't quite place what it was, but I knew it was somehow incomplete, and something told me that once I figured out what, I could very well have the answers needed to shut the case once and for all.

Around lunch time, during a much-appreciated lull in customers, I left Trixie in charge of the store and headed out to do a little more snooping. The next person on my crinkled old list of names to chat with was Bill Sweeney, senior pastor at the First Church of Christmas. I found him in his study in the admin building on the church campus, poring over his notes for the upcoming Christmas Eve service.

"Tom! It's good to see you." Pastor Bill stood and extended a hand across his desk, which was cluttered with papers, opened Bible commentaries, a torn bag of Red Vines licorice twists, and three near-empty coffee mugs. Only one of the mugs still produced swirls of steam. "Take a seat." He gestured toward one of the chairs across from his desk.

Placing my derby hat atop my cane, I set them in the umbrella rack on the pastor's coat stand and complied with his request. He sat down again and leaned back in his oversize office chair. "So, how's Trixie doing?"

"As well as can be expected, I guess," I told him. "I don't know why I'm surprised you knew about it already, but man. News of this is traveling faster than I would have thought possible, even for Christmas."

Bill chuckled. "Heard it from Thelma Smart. No matter how many sermons I preach against gossip, that's one bad habit that woman just can't seem to shake." He paused to grab a stick of licorice and bit into it. "Of course, the detectives showing up at the church would have been a dead giveaway if Thelma hadn't already told the entire congregation."

Thelma Smart was Jonathan Smart's mom. Eli's grandmother. I didn't know she went to this church, since Jonathan had always professed to be Catholic. I just assumed it was a familial thing.

"I can see how that might have been embarrassing for you—the cops showing up here, I mean." I blushed, knowing it was my fault Tice and Lassiter had visited the pastor. I'd given them his name, after all. I decided to skip through any more pleasantries and get right to the business at hand. "Anyway, back to your original question. Yeah, Trixie is doing fine. But as you can imagine, we're trying to sort this whole murder thing out as quickly as we can so she can get back to her life and move on."

"And that's why you've been going around town playing Scooby-Doo? Trying to sniff out the killer, are ya, Tom?" He laughed at this, an overt attempt to let me know he was kidding, but something in the way he said it made me think it wasn't as much of a joke to him as he tried to portray.

"Uh, yeah. Something like that."

"And you want to know if I still have that knife you gave me." I blushed again.

"Yeah, Al told me you'd be coming by and asking about it," Bill said with a grin. "It's no big deal. I understand."

With that, he stood from his desk and strode over to the bookshelf on the other side of the office. I watched as he pulled down a polished-wood shadow box, popped the back open, and brought one of the contents back over to the desk. He then lowered his palm to allow me a look.

In it was a Swiss Army knife, just as shiny as the day it was given to him. A green fir tree rested on the spot where the Swiss Cross normally would be.

The pastor handed the knife to me, then strode around the desk and sat down in his chair again. "Yeah, even though I don't have nearly as much time to play Santa as I used to, that knife was really special to me. I've kept it in that place of honor since becoming the senior pastor here."

I was elated. Both that my old friend cherished the gift that much and that he still had it, effectively eliminating him from my suspect pool. Although, as he said, Bill's duties had pretty much kept him away from his old pals and the Christmas pageantry of Father Christmas, I still considered him one of my dearest friends. I missed spending time with him and his wife, Susan, telling jokes while playing a few hands of Uno together.

I gave the knife one more glance, then set it down on the desk and smiled at my old friend. "So, among all the gossip you've been hearing, anything stand out that might help me figure out who killed Hank?"

Bill took another bite of licorice and glanced at the ceiling in thought before slowly shaking his head. "Um, not really, no. As far as I know, none of my congregation associated with Hank at all. Last thing I remember hearing about him before his death was..."

He paused, his eyes growing wide as he looked at me.

"What? What did you remember?"

"Oh. Wow." He munched down the rest of the licorice stick in thought. "I didn't think anything about it at the time, but in hindsight...wow."

"What? Come on, Bill." I leaned forward in my chair. "Just spit it out."

"It's something Thelma told me." He munched on the bits of licorice in his mouth, his jaw moving side to side slowly. "Something her grandson, Eli, had overheard Hank discussing with Mallory O'Hare just the other day, in fact."

I remembered Eli telling me about the argument he'd seen

Hank having with Mallory, but he'd said he couldn't hear any of the details. Was that a lie? And if so, why?

"For crying out loud, Bill! You're killing me here."

The pastor's face dimmed. His brows furrowed, and he shook his head as he looked me square in the eye. "It's about Trixie, Tom. Hank and Mallory were arguing about Trixie."

16

S o, Al told you about that, huh?" George Trabor said as he slouched back in his chair. His mouth drooped slightly while he shook his head. "Dang, I was hopin' people would have let that go after all this time."

I was sitting in George's living room, watching my old friend squirm uncomfortably in his chair.

Despite the renewed surge of snow, the roads had been surprisingly free from ice as I'd wound my way through the back roads of Christmas to George Trabor's vast farmland property. Among the maelstrom of questions and doubts I'd endured the last few days about the murder, there had been one that had outweighed them all.

Putting aside the major shocker that Bill had told me about Trixie, I'd come to talk to George about Alphonso Garcia's claim that he, George, was a convicted murderer from years before I knew him.

And here I was. After making sure Margaret was well outside of earshot, I'd bluntly asked my question about his previous murder conviction—and regretted it almost instantly. The look on his face when the words poured from my lips spoke volumes. First, I knew instantly that it was true, before he'd even responded. Second, I knew without a doubt that I'd broken his heart by the implied accusation.

After a moment of silence, George nodded. "It's true. I killed a man back in the day, but I ain't proud of it. I don't talk about it none, but Al wasn't lyin' to you."

I felt a lump grow in my throat, constricting the airway and threatening to suffocate me on the spot.

"W–what happened?" The words scraped out from my mouth as if each syllable had snagged against lips made of sandpaper. "If you don't mind my asking."

George let out a sigh, then craned his head around the high back of his armchair to see if his wife was nearby. He stood and waved for me to follow. "Come on," he said. "I've got some work to do before the show tonight. I'll tell you all about it while we work."

Five minutes later, each of us pushing wheelbarrows filled with yards upon yards of Christmas lights, we strolled across George's snow-swept acreage toward the field where his bonfire would be set later that night. It was a time-honored tradition among most of the Santas around here to host a special holiday party bonfire during the days before Christmas, and tonight was George's turn.

"I was young," he said, maneuvering his wheelbarrow over the crunching snow. His sudden segue back into our conversation surprised me, but I kept silent, wanting him to tell his tale in his own way. "In my early twenties, and just discharged from my four-year enlistment in the Army."

I glanced back at the house, thinking of Margaret, and George's desire to talk where she wouldn't hear.

"Oh, she knows all about it," George said, as if reading my thoughts. "I didn't want her knowing you'd asked me about it. She loves you, but I didn't want her thinkin' you were accusing me of anything."

I shook my head. "I'm not," I told him. "Honestly. But after Al told me about it, I had to ask. Have to follow all the leads, wherever they go, if it'll..."

"If it'll get Trixie off the hook. I understand." He shrugged, nearly tipping the wheelbarrow over with the gesture. "Just afraid Margaret wouldn't."

I let that sink in, shivered away a gust of frigid wind, and nodded for him to continue his story.

"Back in those days, I was a bit of a hell-raiser. And just so you know, before I went to the Army, in my high-school years, Hank had been my best friend and we pretty much hell-raised together."

"So, before his wife, Hank was..."

"Pretty much the same as after Ellie left him, yeah. In fact, she had a lot to do with his changing his ways. Getting his act together. Playing Santa Claus and being a good father to Trixie. When she left, so did her influence over him." He sighed. "But you want to hear about the murder I committed."

"Look, George," I said. "If this is too hard for you..."

He held up a callused hand. "No, no. You need to know this. The reason I thought it important to tell you about my relationship with Hank when we were kids was because it was partially his fault I killed Jake Lester that night."

"Hank's fault?"

George nodded just as we came to a stop at the fire pit. It was starting to snow again, and already our tracks leading from his house were being covered up.

Reaching into the wheelbarrow, George grabbed a line of lights and handed one end to me. Together, we set to work untangling the cords while he continued with his story.

"I'd only been home about a week. I'd served—in the

Infantry, mind you—during a time of peace. The Vietnam War had ended 'bout five years before I joined up. Here I was, a tough-as-nails soldier. Killing was the only real skill I'd ever learned well, and I'd never once fired a rifle in a real combat situation. When I came home, I was fit to be tied. Pent up with piss and vinegar, and no means of doin' anything other than farming or ditch-digging. My future wasn't very bright, to say the least."

"Okay." I wasn't sure where his story was heading, and it sounded to me like my old friend was already setting up a tapestry of excuses for the murder. If he was, then I truly didn't know George Trabor the way I thought I did.

"Anyway, that night, Hank, who I hadn't seen since our high school graduation, came over to my house, insistin' we go tear up the town. Hit some bars. Sow some wild oats. Since I didn't have anything better going on in my life, I agreed." He paused. "Now keep in mind, Hank was just as much a mean S.O.B. back then as he was in his later years. Maybe even more so than you or Trixie are aware of. He already had an arrest record longer than my arm. I knew it wasn't a good idea to hang out with him, but we'd always had a lot of fun together back in school, and I honestly needed to do something to blow off steam."

The first batch of lights now untangled, the two of us set to work stringing them along the stand of trees encircling the clearing.

"I didn't know it at the time, but Hank had an ulterior motive for getting me to go out with him that night."

"What kind of ulterior motive?"

"Seems he had a thing for a girl, Ellie Farnsworth."

"Trixie's mom? Your murder conviction had to do with Trixie's mom?" The coincidences were continuing to stack up like a big pile of Margaret's pancakes.

"The very same," he said.

I never really knew Ellie Cobb well. Although Hank and Trixie came into the shop a lot back then, Ellie was either hard at work at her waitressing job or at home, tending house. At first, from what I understand, she was a wonderful wife and an even better mom. She lived to take care of her family, and they all seemed so happy back then. But, one day at work, she slipped on a wet floor and hurt her back. She'd been given pain pills by her doctors and quickly got hooked on them. She went from Oxycontin to Fentanyl to heroin in a span of a couple of years. Then, one day, while nine-year-old Trixie was away at school, she'd packed up her stuff and left without so much as a word. Rumor has it that she took off with her employer, who had disappeared around the same time. But since no one had heard from her since, there was no way to know for sure.

"Let me tell you, she was quite the looker back then, too," George continued. "She'd been prom queen and head cheerleader throughout high school. It was a well-known fact that the girl was adopted, but that didn't seem to hamper her popularity. Every guy in town tried to court her, but only one guy seemed to have any success at it."

"Let me guess. That Jake Lester guy you mentioned."

He tapped the side of his nose with his forefinger and nodded. "Jake and Ellie were at Stuart's Pub. Hank already knew they were there. He figured he'd have a better shot at making his move on her if he could get Jake out of the picture."

"And an old friend fresh out of the Infantry was a perfect wingman."

"Exactly. Long story short, Hank started a fight with the big lug he couldn't possibly win. I jumped in, and my training took over. I ended up stabbing him. Perforated a lung, which filled up with blood, and he died before they could get him to the hospital. Because of the circumstances and my military service, I was convicted of manslaughter and spent six years in prison while Hank walked scot-free. Needless to say, despite both our work in the Santa industry, me and him weren't ever as close after that."

And there it was. Motive. A vise-like pressure gripped my heart as I pondered his story. Six long years spent in a state prison while his puppeteer remained at large, free as a bird. Revenge plots for a lot less had been conceived throughout the years. It wouldn't have taken much to push anyone in George's situation into an act of vengeance. Hank ripping George off might have been the final straw.

"Fortunately, it was in prison where I met Margie," George continued, unaware of the dark thoughts brewing in my head. "She worked part-time as a nurse there. One winter, I caught one of the worst flus of my life. Turned into full-blown pneumonia, and she nursed me back to health. During that time, we got to know each other pretty well. Fell in love. That woman changed my life, and as soon as I was released we got married."

I looked over at him, my mouth agape. I'd never known how he and his wife had met, but this story changed everything. He actually saw his incarceration as a blessing. The turning point in his life, all thanks to Margaret.

I opened my mouth to speak, but he cut me off.

"So, no," he said. "Hank may have left me high and dry to take the fall, but I didn't kill him. It was the best thing that ever happened to me. While I still fret over taking that poor man's life—I'm working hard to atone for it now, by the way—there's no telling where I would have ended up if I hadn't gone to prison."

"I—I..." I looked at him, certain my own guilt was plastered all over my face. "I'm sorry, George. I honestly hoped I was wrong, but..."

"But you had to know for sure." He waved me off. "Like I said, I understand. You'd do anything to protect Trixie, and I don't blame you one bit. That girl's mighty special. I would be doing the same thing if I were in your shoes."

He paused a moment before digging into his jeans pockets. "And if that's not enough to convince you, there's this."

He withdrew a red pocketknife, holding it up so I could see the bright green Christmas tree embedded into the casing. My jaw dropped at the sight.

"I heard how you've been asking all of us about it through your investigation." He laughed, tossing the knife in the air with a little flip and catching it again. "I just figured I'd beat ya to the punch."

I smiled at him, thankful for his friendship, and his patience with me. I was elated. With the presence of George's knife, I could now rule him out as a suspect.

We finished hanging the first strand of lights, then moved on to the next.

"One thing I don't understand," I said out of the blue. Something he'd just told me had been eating at me while we worked. Something that jibed with what I'd just been told by Bill Sweeney. "You mentioned that Ellie Cobb was adopted."

George clicked at his staple gun, securing another piece of string lights to a tree. "Yeah, her mother gave her up the moment she was born."

I nodded. "And her real mother...any idea who she was?"

He stopped for a moment and glanced over at me through hooded eyes. "Something tells me you already know the answer to that."

"So, it's true? Mallory O'Hare, the wealthiest woman in Christmas, is Trixie's grandmother?"

"As you can imagine, not many people know that," George said. "In fact, only five people on Earth should know. Ellie, Hank, me, Margie, and Mallory. We were paid handsomely to keep it a secret." He cocked his head curiously. "I'm just trying to figure out how you know."

I told him about my meeting with the pastor and what Eli had overheard at Mallory's mansion a few days before Hank's death. He whistled in response.

"Oh, boy," he said. "Mallory's not going to like that. She's put in a lot of work to keep the townsfolk in the dark about her little tryst that resulted in Trixie's mom. Not to mention the fact that Trix is heir apparent to Mallory's fortune."

"So, how did *you* find out about it?" I asked him. "If Mallory had kept such a tight rein on her secret for so long, how did *anyone* find out?"

"That was Hank's doing," George said. "There'd been clues as to Ellie's birth mother since she was a child. Certain rules her adopted parents had had to abide by—including staying in Christmas—and other such things that Hank felt were suspicious. He started digging. When I got out of prison, I was reluctantly dragged into his little investigation. Then, one day, it all fell into place. Hank confronted Mallory, and she paid him off. When she found out that I'd helped, she gave me enough money to buy this property outright."

I mulled that over for a moment.

"Think any of this played a part in Hank's death?"

"Dunno. I don't see how. Ain't like Mallory is spry enough in her step—when she's not knee-deep in martinis, that is—to kill a man with a little pocketknife."

He wasn't wrong there. Mallory was approaching seventy-five years of age. She was a wisp of a woman. Barely a hundred pounds, if that. However, she was certainly capable of hiring someone to do it if she chose. But then, how did the Christmas knife come into play? I'd certainly never given her one.

Still, despite the knife issue, my heart pounded against my chest. The case had just opened up a whole new set of possibilities. One that didn't include any of my friends. One with a real, honest-to-goodness motive. One I felt I could really sink my teeth into—although I'd be lying if I didn't admit to a little bias seeping through at the thought of that vicious, miserable woman behind bars. Tamping down my excitement, I impatiently finished helping George set up the rest of the Christmas lights, said my good-byes, and hopped into my car to drive straight to the O'Hare estate.

17

I was driving in a fugue, my mind preoccupied with the news I'd just learned from George. By the time I realized I hadn't been concentrating on the road—and the almost impenetrable cascade of snow falling now—I was halfway to Mallory O'Hare's place.

My foot tapped on the brake to slow down, and I took a breath to calm my nerves. I'd been going at least forty-five miles per hour, which was dangerous enough along this road at the best of times. Not to mention the foolishness of letting your mind wander in near-blizzard conditions. The thought that I'd already driven four and a half miles without so much as a thought on the road was enough to rattle my nerves. I was fortunate I'd not driven into a ditch, or worse, struck some unsuspecting motorist.

Then again, by the looks of traffic—of which I was the only car in sight—the chances against that last thing happening were astronomical.

I leaned forward in the driver's seat, peering carefully out the windshield as both hands gripped the steering wheel tight. I was now driving a safer twenty-five miles per hour, but even at that speed I knew it wasn't a good idea to be out and about. Living in Florida, car tires weren't equipped for the hazards of ice or snow. Not to mention the fact that Florida drivers weren't accustomed to it. I decided at that point to postpone my trip to Mallory's and head back to the shop. I could always speak to the old biddy when the weather lightened up.

At the next intersection, I came to a stop, looked both ways, and made a left-hand turn to head back home. It was just past two p.m., but even now the streetlights were on, trying in vain to illuminate the road as best they could. All they managed to accomplish, however, was to cause the flakes of snow to reflect back their light, making visibility even worse.

I contemplated pulling over entirely, but the shop was just a few more blocks away. I'd made it this far, I figured, so a little farther wouldn't be too difficult.

One of these days I'm going to learn to listen to my instincts.

Driving south on Cupid Street to Comet Avenue, there was nothing on either side of me but miles and miles of ditchwork, fencing to keep deer from crossing the roads, and the wall of evergreens of the Ocala National Forest. So, imagine my surprise when a full-sized pickup truck appeared around the bend ahead, its headlights on high beams, drifting nonchalantly into my lane.

I tensed, honked my horn, and flashed my lights to get the driver's attention, but he didn't move out of my way. I tried slowing down, but the truck accelerated toward me without so much as a swerve.

"...the heck are you doing?" I shouted, trying to think fast.

The road along that stretch had obviously not been traveled much today, as the snow had almost entirely covered the pavement. I could no longer tell where my lane started and the truck's lane ended. Worse, I couldn't tell where the shoulder of the road emptied into the many culverts or ditches along the way.

I flashed my lights again. The driver of the truck flashed theirs right back at me.

Is he drunk, or just being a jerk?

But the truck picked up speed again. It charged straight at me, and I was out of time. By instinct, I jerked the wheel sharp to my right. My Thunderbird swerved out of the pickup's path at the last minute. It was only then that I realized my mistake. The shoulder was narrow. My tires hit gravel, then wet, snow-covered grass. My car spun out from under me, and I found myself rotating counterclockwise for a hundred and eighty degrees, before crashing into the three-foot-deep ditch.

I had just enough time to catch a glimpse of the rusted-out white Ford F-150 as it drove past, along with the hoodie-wearing driver, before the world went dark.

I woke up, uncertain where I was and too afraid to open my eyes to check. My body ached all over; and I couldn't be sure, but I was convinced that my head was no longer attached to the rest of my body. Of course, I knew that was a ridiculous notion. After all, I doubted that I would have been able to even have a ridiculous notion if it was true.

So, as I lay back in what I guessed was a bed of some kind, I knew for a fact that my head was indeed still hooked up with the rest of me.

Time to test the other appendages.

I focused on my fingers. They moved, despite a general stiffness about them. Both hands seemed to work. My toes and feet were the same, though a shock wave of pain lashed down my right shin, just below the knee.

"Tom?"

It was a female voice. A familiar female voice.

"Tom? Are you awake?"

"I'm...I'm not sure." And I wasn't.

The voice wasn't the only noise I heard around me. There was the constant murmur of people speaking softly outside what I assumed was my room. The sound of squeaking wheels rolling down a long hallway. The high-pitched beep of a heart monitor nearby.

I was in a hospital.

I opened my eyes. I couldn't quite focus, so I blinked.

Trixie and Ursula stood next to my hospital bed to my right, smiling down at me. Trixie was clutching a teddy bear with a heart in its paws that was attached to a half-dozen helium balloons exhorting me to "Get Well Soon!"

I smiled at her and nodded to the bear. "Is that for me?"

She shrugged it away with a fake pout. "Get your own teddy bear. This one's mine." Her face cracked into a grin, and she laid the bear next to me on the bed. "You had me freaking out, old man," she continued. "When that FHP trooper showed up at the shop and told me you'd been in a wreck..."

She couldn't finish her thought, turned her back to me, and sniffed.

"You had us all worried," Ursula said, giving my shoulder a gentle pat. I was surprised she'd chosen the one part of my body that didn't seem to be on fire at that moment.

I smiled at her too. I appreciated her concern. It was something I didn't deserve, considering what I'd done to her.

"How long have I been out?" It was the only response I could think of.

"Several hours." Ursula pointed over to the digital clock on the nightstand. "It's just after 10 p.m."

"And the prognosis?"

"Both the FHP and doctors say you're lucky to be alive," she said. "No broken bones. A laceration to your scalp. Your leg is skinned up pretty good where it got pinned under your dashboard. Except for the scalp thing, you didn't receive any head trauma—not even a concussion, which flummoxed the doctors, considering that that heap of yours doesn't have airbags and you weren't wearing a seat belt. Apparently, they're only holding you a little while longer for observation, and said you'd be released around midnight if everything looks good then."

Well, that was good news at least.

"Do you remember what happened?" Ursula asked. "The troopers were pretty sketchy on the details."

I looked around my bed for the remote control and raised the mattress up to look her in the eyes. "Just some nutjob driving on the wrong side of the road," I said.

"It was snowing," she reminded me. "The roads were covered, so maybe he didn't realize he was in the wrong lane."

I shook my head and told her the story of my ride from George Trabor's. "Despite numerous attempts to warn him with my headlights, he just flashed his right back at me and kept on coming." I paused. "And I've seen that truck before."

"That's disturbing," she said. "Where?"

"Yesterday. When I was over at Teddy Gorshon's. It drove past real slow, like it was looking for something. I didn't think anything of it at the time, but now..."

Trixie spun around. "You don't think it was a warning, do you?"

I looked at her. "A warning?"

"Yeah. Like, the killer knows you're investigating Hank's murder, and you're getting too close," she explained. "Maybe he's warning you to stay out of it or something."

I glanced over at Ursula, who shrugged. "It's a possibility," I said, "but it felt like more than a warning to me. The way he was driving, I think the guy decided to skip the warning and take me out of the picture altogether."

Now that I really thought about it, something didn't feel right to me. First, until I talked to George and learned about the strange relationship between Hank and Mallory, as well as the fact that Trix could be Mallory's granddaughter—something I wasn't going to share with anyone just yet—I hadn't gotten "too close" at all. In fact, I'd just been spinning my wheels. Just as confused as the day I found Hank dead. Hardly anything worthy of a warning, much less trying to kill me. I wasn't much of a threat to anyone.

I looked down at my body, covered in a hospital gown and blankets, then over at Ursula. "Where's my suit?"

"You can't leave yet. The doctors aren't ready to let you go."

"You're my attorney," I told her. "Can they hold me here against my will?"

She paused for a moment. "Well, no, but..."

I sat up in my bed and carefully maneuvered my legs around to the edge. "I don't feel like waiting around. I'd rather rest in my own bed." I turned my attention to Trixie. "What did they do with my suit?"

"It's over there in the closet." She nodded across the room.

"Tom, your suit is ruined," Ursula protested. "It was covered in the blood from your head wound and your scraped-up shin. Plus, the nurse told me it was pretty much in tatters. Shredded mostly when the EMTs were trying to pull you from the car."

Ignoring her, I kept my eyes on Trix. "Can you get it for me?"

She nodded, then walked over to the closet, opened it, and came back to the bed with a perfectly fine, bright green and red checkered suit with red bow tie. Ursula blinked for a moment, then turned to Trixie. "How did you bring him a new suit without my knowing?"

The young Goth grinned up at her, then offered me a wink. I smiled back at her and motioned for the two of them to give me some privacy. Trixie knew the truth. It was, indeed, the same suit I'd been wearing at the time of the crash. But just as it had magical pockets that could hold any assortment of items that could fit through their openings, it also had the unique quality of always staying clean, pressed, and ready to wear. That's quite handy on those days I just can't bring myself to run to the dry cleaners.

Five minutes later, I was dressed to impress and walking down the hospital corridor with my two favorite ladies beside me. I was leaving against medical advice, but that was my prerogative. Besides, I had a murderer to catch, and I was slowly coming to realize that there was much more to the death of Hank Cobb than I had originally perceived.

18

I awoke the next morning in my own bed, filled with the same aches and pains as the night before. For nearly ten minutes I lay there, looking up at the wood-paneled ceiling above my king-sized bed, dreading the effort it would take to slip from my warm, cozy covers and into the mess my life had become over the last few days.

"Pep?" I asked. "You there?"

"Of course I am, you beanpole. I'm always here, thanks to the inhumane binding you have on me."

I rolled my eyes, not wanting to remind him that (a) it wasn't me who bound him to the House, and (b) it was his impish flare for mischief that had landed him in his current position to begin with. If I could trust him more, I might be inclined to release him one day. But he still had to earn that trust, and he was nowhere close to doing that anytime soon.

"Will you open the curtains for me?" I asked, ignoring his complaint entirely.

With an exasperated sigh, he swung the thick light-blocking curtains back from the window, unleashing the full brunt of the sun into my otherwise dim room. I blinked away tears as the sunlight pelted me with its brilliant rays.

"I take it that it's stopped snowing?"

"For now," the elf answered. "Though there's about two feet of the stuff on the ground."

Two feet? Geez.

"Must be some kind of record," I said, climbing out of bed, shuffling over to the bathroom, and loading my toothbrush with paste.

"Last time I saw this much snow on the ground here, the white man hadn't even touched the shores of Florida yet," he told me. "Ah, those were the days. The Seminole practically worshiped me as a god, ya know. They certainly didn't treat me like some sort of unpaid butler."

I stopped brushing my teeth in mid-stroke and spit into the sink. "Okay, what's going on, Pep? Why the pity party all of a sudden?"

I looked out the bathroom door into my bedroom to see the foot of my bed sink down a bit.

"Horatio never had people murdered inside the House," he said. His voice wasn't so much accusatory as it was genuinely sad. "He never went out trying to catch killers, and such."

I rinsed the toothpaste from my mouth and strode back into the room. "It's not exactly my fault that Hank Cobb was killed. I'm not sure what you're getting at, Peppermint."

He sighed again. I could almost hear him shrug his shoulders. "It's just that so much has changed in the last few years. You know as well as anybody, elves don't get on with change very well. And then there's the matter of Horatio's promise to me."

I was now buttoning my pants and slipping on my suit coat, and it hit me. It was the same thing on this day, every year. I'd forgotten. Horatio had made a promise to Peppermint. If the elf behaved himself—showed that he could be beneficial to the world at large and contain his impish inclinations—he would take Pep's case to the Krin'Ghal. He would petition the Spirit of Christmas to release him from his House bond. But my predecessor had died, leaving the estate, as well as the mantle of Santa-in-Training, to me; and all the elf's hard work had been thrown out the window. Especially considering that Peppermint and I had never exactly gotten along.

"I've been stuck in this House for a hundred and fifty-two years, Nast," Peppermint continued, his voice now coming from the northeast window. "Haven't so much as seen the outside world from beyond your silly little parking lot out there."

The pane of glass fogged up just a tad as the elf breathed against it.

"And," he continued, "since you never agreed to Horatio's promise, I suppose I won't see the outside world anytime soon."

"We've talked about this, Pep," I told him, making the finishing touches to my necktie that sported green and red Christmas-tree balls. "Every year, it's the same thing. Every year, you get depressed and make my life more difficult than it needs to be. I'm more than willing to honor the deal, but you've got to work for it."

"How can I?" he asked. "When all you do is keep me locked away here, day after day. I could be so useful to you in your little investigation, and you know it."

I laughed at this. "No way."

"Why not?"

"Because I'm not letting you out of this House until I know I can trust you. There's no telling what you might—"

My sentence was cut off by the sound of my old mechanical phone shrilling on top of my nightstand. My heart skipped a beat. No one ever called me. There was rarely any need. I picked the receiver off its cradle and lifted it to my ear.

"Hello?"

"Boss?" It was Trixie's voice. "Better get down here. You've got some..." She paused at this. "...unusual visitors here to see you, and they don't look very happy."

"I'll be right down." I hung up the phone, my mind abuzz with all the unpleasant possibilities that awaited me downstairs. I looked around the room, unsure where Peppermint was now positioned. "We'll talk more about this later," I told the air. "I promise."

With that, I limped from my bedroom as best as my scraped shin would allow, down the winding staircase to the first floor, to see three rather formidable-looking gentlemen waiting for me with sour expressions on their block-like faces.

With the Christmas shopping crowd clogging the store, I directed Vinnie Tarturo and his two goons to the kitchen area where we could talk in private.

"Mr. Nast," Tarturo said after taking a seat at the breakfast table. His two men stood behind him, looking nervously around the room. Their eyes darted back and forth at the slightest bit of noise. From the smaller goon's limp as they lumbered into the kitchen, I was fairly certain they were my burglars from two nights earlier—Louis and Jimmy—and I could understand their discomfort. "I want to extend my appreciation for your meeting with us on such short notice."

I opened my mouth to reply, then shut it again. Though the trio was, without a doubt, intimidating, we were in my domain. As the mobster's two toughs knew all too well, they couldn't scare or threaten me while we were within these walls. And, while Tarturo's attempt at pleasantries was appreciated, I wanted to get this over with as soon as possible so I could visit Mallory O'Hare to question her about what I'd learned last night.

Plus, I wanted the gangsters to understand that I was in control of the discussion.

"What can I do for you, Mr. Tarturo?" I asked. "As you can see by my customers out there—" I nodded to the door leading out of the kitchen "—this is my busiest time of the year, and I don't have the time, or the patience, to beat around the bush." I nodded to his men. "Given that your associates broke into my place recently, I assume you want something from me."

The mobster's lips curled into a grin, and he leaned forward on the table. His eyes gleamed like a wolf's stalking a lamb. "As a matter of fact, Mr. Nast, I do. I believe you have something of mine, and I want it back."

I leaned back in my chair, folding my arms across my chest. "Care to share what it is I'm supposed to have?"

"Don't play coy with me, kid," he said, grinding his teeth with each syllable. "Cobb had it right before he died. Since he was killed here in your little shop, it stands to reason that you have it. So, drop the act."

I stared back at him, unwilling to show him the slightest trace of fear. "Maybe the cops have it. They were here an awful long time doing their investigation, and their CSI guys seemed to be pretty good at finding things that didn't want to be found." Now was my time to lean forward and look him square in the eyes. I know mobsters aren't supposed to be warm and fuzzy, but there was something about this man that pushed all my buttons. I didn't like him one bit and made a note in my head to remind Santa to put him on the "Naughty List" if he hadn't already. "Since I've got no idea what it is, and haven't found anything that doesn't belong here, maybe the cops found it and took it as evidence." I waved a hand around dismissively. "It's not like they showed me a receipt of what they took from my store."

I guess Vinnie Tarturo was unaccustomed to having people stand up for themselves around him, because he didn't seem to like my response. He slammed a mallet-like fist down on the breakfast table. "Enough with the games, Nast. Give me my fifty Gs, and I'll see to it you aren't put up in the hospital in traction."

There was a shockwave tremor in the table that had nothing to do with the mobster striking it. Louis tensed, his eyes widening as he glanced over at Jimmy. Jimmy had felt it too.

I smiled. "I'd be careful of making threats to me in my own home, Mr. Tarturo." I gestured toward his men. "Larry and Curly there both know what happens to unwanted guests who irk me."

Vinnie guffawed at this, then leaned even farther across the table. His eyes were like laser beams burning into me. "And I suppose I'm Moe, is that it?"

"You don't have enough hair for his bowl haircut."

I was pushing my luck. The man was a notorious gangster, after all. Granted, rumor had it that he'd been such a poor excuse for one in New York that he'd been shipped down to Christmas to get him out of the Family's way. But he was a gangster nonetheless, and I shouldn't take that as lightly as I was. But I was getting sick and tired of the threats—by both cops and robbers. Tired of not knowing what was going on. Tired of being run off the road by psychos.

And I was getting angry too. Angry over a murder that had taken place within the hallowed halls of my House and my shop. Angry over what it was doing to Trixie.

So, at that moment, I wasn't really in the mood to give the man the respect I might normally.

And he didn't like it one bit.

Vinnie Tarturo reached into his jacket and pulled out a rather large gun before pointing it directly at my face. "Where are the jokes now, Nast?"

There was a pop. I clenched my eyes shut, then heard a reverberating crash and a string of curses from the mobster. Given that I could hear anything at all told me that I was still alive, and I realized the *pop* I'd heard was not the sound of a gun firing, but rather something akin to a miniature black hole opening up and sucking something through. I opened my eyes to find Tarturo flat on his back, his arms and feet in the air like a turtle trying to roll over on the ground. There was no sign of the chair he'd been sitting in only moments before.

"Boss! Boss!" the two men said in unison as they hustled over to their employer, trying to help him to his feet.

"I told ya this place was haunted or somet'in'," the smaller one said. "I told ya!"

"Shut up, Louis," Vinnie said, slapping their hands from his shoulder after he was on his own two feet. He glanced around, searching for something, then looked at me. "What'd ya do with my gun?"

I shrugged. "It's probably in the same place as the chair. My House can be notoriously mischievous when the mood strikes it." I gestured toward the door. "Now, gentlemen, I really must insist that I get back to my customers. Christmas is coming soon, after all."

Tarturo glared at me. Jimmy and Louis flanked both sides of him, still trying to help the big mobster get steady on his feet. He then pointed at me.

"All right, Freak," he said. "I'll give you just twenty-four hours to give me back my money. Then, we ain't gonna be so nice." His eyes darted over to the door, then he smiled. "I'd hate to see any-thing happen to that pretty cashier of yours. You get me?"

My fists clenched at the threat, but I held my cool. House and elf aside, I would be no match for these three. Besides, once I stepped out my door, neither of them would be able to protect me against their wrath. They had me over a barrel. Either I found Vinnie's money, or I would eventually pay for my little display of hubris here today.

I relaxed, then nodded. "I'll try to find it and get it to you as soon as possible. Now, please, leave."

With a gravelly chuckle, the mobster and his goons obeyed, leaving me alone in the kitchen with some very troubling thoughts.

19

just don't think it's here," Ursula said, wiping the sweat from her forehead as she crouched inside an empty cardboard box. "Are you sure it's not upstairs somewhere?"

"I'm positive." I couldn't tell her that the House was off limits past the stairs to all uninvited guests. If someone were to attempt to climb them without permission, they could just as easily find themselves stepping out into the back yard at the first door they stepped through. It's just how the place works.

Trix, Ursula, and I had practically torn the store apart an hour after it had closed, looking for the cash Vinnie Tarturo accused me of having. All the artificial Christmas trees had been stripped bare and taken apart, their fronds lying scattered over the hardwood floor. The empty boxes that had been wrapped like presents had been opened, their festive paper and ribbons now filling five thirty-gallon trash bags sitting near the door.

I was standing with my back to Ursula, holding a divining charm—a pendant connected to a golden chain—hoping it would assist in the search. The charm, given to me by Horatio Longpepper when I first came to work for him, was said to be able to find any lost item within a one-mile radius. So far, it hadn't worked.

Trixie was now leaning back on a divan we had for weary shoppers near the back of the storefront, her feet kicked up on the coffee table. "I don't think it's here either," she said, giving me a knowing look. "You know as well as I that if it was, you would have found it by now."

Translation: the House would have revealed it to us long ago.

And she was right. I knew it. But Tarturo had been so convinced that Hank Cobb had had his money when he'd accosted Trixie at the pub. Was so sure he'd had it when he came into my store after her. But if he'd hidden it somewhere in here, the House was unaware of it...which was impossible.

I took a swig from my water bottle and wiped away the moisture from my own brow. Although it had started snowing again outside, the heat inside the store had been cranked up—thanks in large part to the ladies helping me—to a very uncomfortable eighty degrees. With the physical activity of dismantling the merchandise and displays to search for Tarturo's property, it was stifling inside.

I walked to the front door and opened it, letting the cold outside bombard me with its refreshing breath. It's strange. I'd always hated the cold. It was one of the reasons I'd never looked forward to becoming Santa—not that he actually lived at the North Pole. The vessel of Krin'Ghal resided in another dimension known as Wyndter—which was just as cold, I might add. But the older I grew, the more accustomed I became to the chill. It startled me to realize it, but I was beginning to like it. Which scared me even more because I wondered if the time to accept the mantle of Santa Claus was approaching faster than I would like to admit.

"Trixie's right, and you know it, boss," Peppermint whispered from somewhere near my left knee. I glanced back to check on Ursula, but thankfully she was too busy to notice me talking to myself.

"I know," I told the hob. "But I don't exactly know what else to do. Tarturo made it clear that if I didn't find his money, I wasn't going to like what he'd do." I turned to look back at Trixie. "I'm not as much worried about me, as her."

"I get it," he said. His voice was unusually sincere. "I'd do anything to keep that kid safe. Those pockets of yours can do some pretty amazing things, but they can't conjure items from nowhere. You've got to know where an object is for them to work."

I nodded with a sigh of almost-defeat. I say "almost" because I wasn't quite ready to give up just yet. There had to be a place on the first floor we hadn't thought to look. Or there was a reason the House was secreting the money away from us. I just couldn't quite figure it out.

"You know, Eli might have been right the other day," Ursula said. "Maybe the killer took it? That seems like the most plausible explanation."

"Which means, find the money and we find our killer," Trixie added.

I nodded. The logic was sound. It was as good a possibility as anything, but it got us nowhere closer to finding either than when we'd first started tearing my place apart. I was about to say as much when the phone rang. I closed the door, walked over to the counter, dropped the divining charm in its usual place in a drawer, and answered the phone.

"Hello?" I asked into the receiver.

"T—Tom?" came the shaking voice on the other end of the line. It was a male voice, but I couldn't quite place it.

"Yes, this is Tom Nast. Who is this?"

The caller hesitated.

"Yeah, it's Teddy. Teddy Gorshon." There was a tremble in his voice I didn't like.

"Teddy? Is everything okay? You don't sound—"

"I need to...to talk to you. Soon as possible." He breathed heavy into the mic. "I think I know who killed Hank..."

I tensed at the news, but he seemed to trail off.

"Teddy? What is it? What's going on?"

"You're not going to believe who..." There was a pause. "Wait... what are you doing here? I didn't do nothin' to you. Why are you..."

The phone went dead. When I replaced the receiver on the cradle, Trixie and Ursula were staring at me with concern on their faces. After telling them about the disturbing conversation, I borrowed Ursula's car—the House hadn't quite finished the repairs to my own after the wreck—and hightailed it back out to Teddy Gorshon's place as fast as I safely could in the raging snowstorm we were currently having.

Twenty minutes later, I pulled up next to his Gulf Stream. I was suddenly caught up with an intense feeling of unease. I hadn't liked what I'd heard in that phone conversation at all. Someone had been there with Teddy. Someone he was scared of. Considering that he'd just told me he thought he knew who the murderer was...

I let that thought trail off as I got out of my car. The sun had been down for several hours now and there were no lights on in Teddy's camper. To add to my tension, the property I was on was near Pierson Swamp, a parcel of wetlands that was always teeming with life. But the place was deathly quiet. Even with the wintry storm, there should have been bird calls somewhere in the distance. The buzz of mosquitos at least. Yet now the only sound I could hear were the ice crystals impacting with the accumulating snow and the howl of the wind.

Cautiously, I stepped up to the trailer's door, and knocked. "Teddy? You in there?"

The moment my fist struck the metal door, it bounced against its frame and swung back slowly toward me. Not only was the door unlocked, but it was ajar.

"Ted?"

I eased the door open farther, stood up on the first step, and peered inside. The place was dark. Only a few streams of moonlight peeked in through the curtains to give a modicum of illumination. I glanced around for a moment until my eyes came to rest on the silhouette of a man sitting at the booth in the kitchenette.

"Teddy?" I asked again, but there was no answer. The more I looked at the silhouette, the more I didn't like the angle of it. It was slumped over to the left, as if he was sleeping.

Well, I had heard he'd been drinking again. Maybe he just passed out.

I moved into the camper and flipped the light switch, but the lights refused to turn on. I gave the switch a few more tries, but the room remained veiled in darkness.

My heart thumped against my chest, threatening to rise in my throat. I was liking this situation less and less every second. Reaching into my jacket pocket, my hand searched around until it found what I was looking for. When my hand withdrew, it was holding a powerful twelve-inch-long Maglite. I clicked the flashlight on, and the entire interior of the camper blazed to life.

Instantly, I regretted my ability to see as I gazed over at the body of Teddy Gorshon, with what looked like a rather large bullet hole in his chest.

"Ah, Teddy..." I moved over to the kitchenette where the dead man slouched and checked for a pulse I knew wouldn't be there. Before I could reach him, an explosion from outside nearly shattered my eardrums. Two more loud pops echoed from outside, followed by the ping of metal being punched through by something small and powerful.

I was being shot at!

I dropped to the floor, covering my head with my hands— as if that would do any good whatsoever against the barrage of gunfire—and prayed that my assailant would run out of bullets before any of them struck me.

As you might have figured out, considering that my mentor, Horatio, had died a few years ago, the heir to the Spirit of Christmas is not immortal. We do tend to heal faster than most. We get sick less often and less severely. And we tend to live much longer than average. But a bullet between the eyes can kill me just as easily as your average mortal. The only real protection against violence I have is when I'm in the confines of the House, which is a hub of sorts to the realm of Wyndter, the land of the Krin'Ghal.

After around ten shots punched holes in the thin sheet metal of the camper, letting a little more moonlight in, the world around me grew silent again. I tensed, holding my breath and listening for any movement outside. A moment later, I heard the crunch of snow as someone stalked toward the trailer door. Glancing around for anything I could use for a weapon, I quickly came up short. Nothing nearby would do any good against a gun, and I could only assume my attacker had already reloaded and was now coming to finish the job.

Then I noticed that I was clutching the flashlight in my hands for dear life. The beam of light shone up onto the roof, swishing back and forth in rhythm with the pounding of my heart. I might as well have been brandishing a neon bull's-eye for anyone wanting to take potshots at me.

I flicked the light off, then hefted the flashlight up in my dominant hand. It was hefty, used by many police officers as a baton in a pinch. I smiled grimly, realizing that I had a weapon after all, for what little good it would do me.

There was more crunching of snow, then a shuffle as my attacker came to the doorway. Quietly, I huddled up underneath the kitchenette table, took in one final deep breath, and waited. Some more crunching, then the telltale sign of a boot climbing onto the metal step just outside. A shadow filled the doorframe. A slim hooded figure in the dark. A large-caliber handgun clutched in a gloved hand.

The intruder turned toward the kitchenette, lifting both gun and flashlight in my direction. The beam of the light swept just above my head, leaving me concealed for the moment in the shadows under the table. Then it came back, dipping ever so slightly toward the floor. When it fell on me, it paused. The assassin stopped, steadying the aim of the gun.

Panicked, I did the only thing I could think of. I pressed the button of my own flashlight, bringing its powerful beam to life. The figure, momentarily blinded by the sudden flash, reeled back, bringing their arm up to protect their eyes from the light. With the momentary reprieve, I took aim, and hurled the flashlight at the gunman. It tumbled end over end through the air, striking my attacker in the hand. I heard a crack of bones popping, then a high-pitched cry. The gun dropped from the hand, clattering to the floor. My eyes followed it as it tumbled a few times across the linoleum. When I looked up again, the figure was gone. The only thing remaining was the sound of crunching snow fading in the distance as they ran away.

Soon, I was completely alone with my dead friend slumped over in the booth above my head.

20

Detectives Tice and Lassiter had been none too pleased to see me at another murder scene. They'd grilled me at poor Teddy's trailer for nearly two hours before agreeing to let me go. I'd ended up telling them about the visit I'd had earlier that day from Vinnie Tarturo. How we'd turned my store upside down looking for his stolen money, and how our search had stopped when I'd gotten a call from Teddy asking to see me.

Lassiter, ever playing the role of "good cop," jotted my story down meticulously, all the while commending me on my bravery and quick thinking when being shot at. Tice, who made it clear that he doubted my account was entirely true, merely grunted or chuckled, shaking his head as I told my story. I got the distinct impression that he would have told me not to leave town if cops actually said those kinds of things in real life. Instead, he warned me again about my private investigation and said he'd be in touch. They released me, and I headed straight to Wonderland as fast as was safely possible.

When I entered the shop, I found Ursula standing near the back of the showroom, staring at one of the walls with her mouth hung open like a garage door. She was pale. Her eyes were wide, her pupils dilated. I was no doctor, but from where I stood I could swear she was in shock.

"Ursula?" I walked over to her, touching her shoulder. She jumped before glancing at me, then turned back to look at the wall. I followed her gaze but saw nothing. "Ursula, are you okay?"

When she didn't respond, I took her by the hand and led her over to the customer divan and helped her sit down. I looked around the room for Trixie, but she was nowhere to be seen.

"Hold on a second," I told her, then dashed into the kitchen to put on a kettle of tea. As the kettle began to boil, I hollered for Peppermint. "You here?"

"Aren't I always?"

I ignored his sarcastic reply. "What's going on? Where's Trix? What happened to Ursula?"

The elf harrumphed. "How in blazes should I know?"

"Because, as you say, you're always here." I looked around the room, approximating his location by the sound of his voice, and glared. "Have you been drinking again?"

"Not since the other day," he said. "Booze kind of lost its appeal to me ever since that horrible man was put out of all our misery."

"Pep!"

"Sorry, boss. But no. I don't know what happened. After you left, they pretty much gave up the search and just jabbered away for a little while. Then Trixie said she was going out and would be back soon. And I wasn't about to stay in the same room with Ursula the Hun by myself for any amount of time. I might become as wretchedly depressed as you've been if I did that. So I went to my room and read for a while." There was a pause. "Why? What's happened to the Ice Queen?"

"I'm not sure." The kettle was whistling now. I took it off the stove and poured the steaming liquid into a cup before steeping the tea bag for a few moments. "But something's upset her." I glanced around the kitchen, a terrible thought crossing my mind. "You don't think the House..."

"No..." Peppermint did not sound at all convincing. "Of course not. It wouldn't do that to one of your friends." He hesitated. "Would it?"

I wasn't so sure. The House had been acting mighty weird lately, especially after the murder. It had started with the indoor snowstorm the other day. The rumbling. The attack on the burglars—which I guess wasn't so strange when I thought about it. And Vinnie Tarturo's disappearing chair. But besides the snow, the other incidents had all been directed toward people hostile to me. I could see no reason for it to do something to Ursula. Sure, she'd broken my heart, but Ursula wasn't even aware she'd done that. It was in the past. And I was pretty sure the House didn't really hold grudges. If it did, Peppermint wouldn't have simply been turned into the House's servant: he would have gotten a much more suitable comeuppance a long time ago.

Once the tea was ready, I made two cups, placed them both on saucers, and carried them over to Ursula, who was craning her head for a better look at the wall she'd been staring at earlier.

"What are you looking for?" I asked, setting her tea on the coffee table in front of her.

She jumped at the sound of my voice and turned to look at me. There was already a little more color spreading through her cheeks, and she blinked.

"I saw..."

"What?" I asked, taking a sip of my own tea. "What did you see?"

She shook her head. "Never mind. It's crazy."

"Seriously. Tell me. What did you see?"

She turned to look at the wall one more time, then turned

her attention back to me. She picked up her cup and took a sip. She seemed to be quickly coming out of her stupor.

"It really is very silly now that I think about it."

"Just tell me." I took her free hand in mine and gave it a comforting squeeze.

"Well, Trixie left a while back, leaving me alone since you had my car."

"Sorry about that."

She waved it away. "Sometime later, Eli came by to check on Trixie." She sighed. "That boy has a huge crush on her, you know."

"That he does," I agreed.

"Anyway, while he was here, we talked for a while. We discussed Trixie's case a bit, and I told him about Vinnie Tarturo's missing money. He figured we could kill some time until Trixie came back by continuing the search, so we started looking some more." She stopped, looking around the shop. Her eyes widened again as she realized that the trees, presents, displays, and decorations were already back in their proper places. "How...did..."

"Go on," I urged her, trying to take her mind off how the shop had mysteriously reassembled itself. The first time she'd learned about the true nature of the House—about me—she hadn't handled it that well. It's why her memory had been wiped. I didn't want to repeat that ordeal ever again, especially with everything else that was going on at the moment. "You were looking for the stuff..."

"Yeah, we were looking for it, and all of a sudden, I heard a growl."

Tinsel. My brow furrowed.

"I guess Eli heard it too, so we started looking for the source of the growling. It was a strange sort of noise. Not like a dog or cat or anything like that. I can't really describe it."

"Okay."

"Anyway, Eli was standing just over there." She pointed to the wall she'd been staring at. "He started shouting, then just ran out of the store and drove off. I could hear him screaming all the way to his truck." She took another sip of tea and brushed a strand of hair from her face before continuing. "Anyway, I was curious as to what had frightened him so much, so I walked over to where he'd been, and then I saw it..."

Her voice trailed off. Her eyes sort of glazed over, as if staring into some great abyss.

"Saw what, Ursula? What did you see?"

She didn't need to tell me. I knew exactly what it was, and I was flooded with a mix of conflicting emotions at the thought. On the one hand, I was irritated with the alligator for threatening my friends, people who had every right to be in the House. On the other hand, I was annoyed that everyone else seemed to have laid their eyes on the reptilian monster but me, and I was supposed to be the master of the House, which meant I was the alligator's master as well. And yet, no matter how many times I've tried, I've never been able to lay my eyes on so much as a scale of the thing.

"It was just a glimpse, mind you," she said. "Probably a trick of the light or something. But I could have sworn that I saw the tip of a long alligator tail."

And there it was. My suspicions confirmed. And yet I would need to deny such a sighting while also sparing her feelings while I did it. It wouldn't do to make her feel insecure or, worse, insane. It wasn't the first time she'd seen Tinsel. Besides Trixie, Ursula had seen him more times than anyone I knew. In fact, the way I hear it, he's taken quite a shine to her, if you can believe Peppermint's account. Of course, those encounters had been erased from her memory as well.

"You're right," I heard myself say, then quickly covered. "I mean, about the lighting. The lights in here do some crazy things with my eyes all the time. Shadows here and there, then some Christmas lights flash, and it makes the shadows look as though they're moving. I could easily imagine seeing something that looked like a long slithery tail in some of the corners around here."

She turned around and looked over at the wall again before shaking her head. "There seems to be a lot of lighting over there. Not that many shadows at all."

"But if there was an alligator there, where did it go? There's not exactly a gator door cut into the wall, now is there?"

"Well, that's the really weird thing," she answered. "It looked...for that split second, mind you...that it simply walked through the wall and disappeared."

I stared at her, not wanting to argue with her. She was no doubt correct, but I still couldn't assure her of that. So, with nothing of any use that I could possibly say to ease her mind, I simply stared at her. She immediately misinterpreted my silence.

She threw up her hands, nearly sloshing the remaining tea in her cup all over the Persian carpet the divan sat on. "I told you it was crazy. Knew you wouldn't believe me."

"No, no, it's not that. I think you really did see something. It's just that—"

"What time is it?" she interrupted me.

"Huh?"

"What time is it? Trixie's been gone an awful long time, and I'm starting to get worried about her."

I pulled my watch fob from my vest pocket and popped it open. "One thirty." Geez, the detectives had kept me at Teddy's place a lot longer than I'd actually realized. "When did she leave here?"

Ursula shrugged. "Not long after you. Maybe five or ten minutes. Tops."

I thought about that for a moment. From law enforcement's point of view, it didn't sound good. Leaving five or ten minutes after I did would have given her plenty of time to get to Teddy's and open fire on me. I didn't believe she would, mind you. Besides the fact that I loved her like my own daughter, and I was pretty sure the feeling was mutual, she didn't have a car. But Seth Timmons did. If Trixie had set the whole thing up, she would have needed an accomplice. Someone to get to Teddy after he called me and kill him before I arrived. And Seth was obsessed enough with the girl that I could easily see him doing whatever she asked of him.

Come to think of it, take Trix out of the equation completely and maybe Seth was obsessed enough with her to take some initiative without her knowledge. Knowing the painful past she had with her father, what if Seth had killed Hank Cobb? Then, while investigating the murder, he perceived me as a threat, and...

No, the very notion was preposterous. First, Seth Timmons was a world-class stoner. Lazy to the core. And let's face it, not the brightest bulb in any pack. He'd hardly be "criminal mastermind" material. I just couldn't see it.

Still, the idea of Trixie leaving and her whereabouts unknown at the time I was being attacked was something I would have to keep from Detective Tice if at all possible. The detective had very little imagination, and I doubt he'd flesh out his suspicions the way I just had. He'd be just as likely to lock her up for attempted murder on me, just to be done with the case.

Besides, I was beginning to suspect that there was something I was missing about Hank Cobb's murder. There was a nudge in the back of my mind that told me there was more to this story than I currently knew. I couldn't explain why, but something was definitely troubling me about the whole affair. And then, of course, there was his Santa suit. Something still nagged me about it as well.

"Tom?"

I looked over at Ursula, who was staring at me with a curious look. "Huh?"

"I asked you if we should call her to see if she's okay."

"Oh." I blinked away my embarrassment of not having been paying attention to her. "Sorry. I was thinking. But yeah, calling her would be a good idea."

I stood up and made my way over to the counter and the good old-fashioned landline telephone and picked up the receiver. There were maybe two other people I knew, besides me, who still memorized phone numbers, and Trixie's was number one on my mental speed dial.

As it rang on my end, I heard Trixie's ring tone blaring the musical score of "What's This?" from *The Nightmare Before Christmas* just out the front door. A moment later, the door swung open and Trixie walked into the shop, stomping her feet and shaking the snow from her knee-high boots and red- and green-streaked raven hair. In one of her hands, she carried an old army-issued duffel bag, which she proceeded to set down on the counter before shrugging out of her coat.

"Geez!" she said, tossing the coat over the chair behind the counter. "It's freakin' freezing out there!"

I looked from her to the duffel, then pointed. "Um, what'cha got there, Trix?"

I had a feeling that I already knew the answer.

She beamed at me, confirming my suspicions. With her back to Ursula, she held up the divining pendant for the briefest of seconds, then tucked it away back in the drawer. When Ursula rounded the counter, Trixie unzipped the duffel to reveal several stacks of hundred-dollar bills.

"How on Earth did you find that?" Ursula asked, riffling through the stacks of money, which I estimated to be nearly a hundred grand.

But that didn't make sense. Vinnie said Hank had only stolen about fifty. Where did the rest of the cash come from?

Trixie gave a coy shrug to Ursula's query. "Well, I realized the money couldn't possibly be in the house. It would surely have"— she looked over at me with a knowing look—"materialized by now if it was.

"After Tom left to go see Teddy, I got to thinking about that night. The night my father approached me at the pub, when he followed me out to the parking lot. I remembered. He was carrying a duffel bag at the time. He tossed it down on the ground when we started arguing. I figured the parking lot would be a good place to maybe look for it."

"So that's where you found it?" I asked. I couldn't believe something like a discarded bag full of cash would go unmolested for long. One of the patrons would surely have looked inside it.

And that's when it hit me. I knew exactly what had happened next before Trixie even needed to tell me. "Jose Jimenez."

Trixie gave me a wink while pointing finger guns at me. "Bingo."

"Wait," Ursula said. "I don't understand. Was the bag at the pub, or not?"

Trix shook her head. "No, it wasn't. But that's because the one witness to our argument..."

"Jose Jimenez," I added. "The guy who reported it to the police that got Trix in trouble to begin with."

"Exactly," Trixie said.

"So, what?" Ursula asked. "Could he have followed Mr. Cobb here, killed him, and took the bag? Could Jimenez be our killer?"

"I don't know," I said. "Unless he knew what was in it, why would he have bothered? It doesn't make a whole lot of sense."

"Well, that's something else I remembered from that night," Trixie said. "Hanky followed me about a block, begging me to give him a chance. He left the bag. He didn't have it with him when I finally told him to leave me alone. I ran away then and didn't see if he went back for the bag or not. But something told me he kept following me. How else would he know I went to the store instead of my apartment? If he did, then he *couldn't* have gone back for the bag. He wouldn't have had the time."

Ursula looked at Trixie. "Wait. How exactly did you find the bag? Does Jimenez know you have it?"

This is where the Goth's pale complexion turned three different shades of red. She tilted her head slightly, and I knew she was about to tell me something I wasn't going to like. I could surmise how she'd actually found the bag: she'd taken the divining charm. All she would have had to do was use it within a mile of the loot, and she'd find it.

"Trix? Answer the nice lawyer's question."

"You're not going to like the answer."

"I'm pretty sure I'm not. Tell me anyway."

She glanced from me to Ursula, then let out a deep sigh. "Okay. So, I figured that Jose would want to keep that kind of money pretty safe and well hidden, but not at his house. Especially if he suspected where it might have come from."

"Why would he even suspect it came from Vinnie Tarturo?" Ursula asked.

"Because Jose occasionally works for Vinnie," Trixie explained. "He runs a chop shop in Orlando, and rumor is it's owned by Vinnie."

My eyes widened. This was news to me, and it bothered me that my protégé was still very much "in the know" when it came to the criminal enterprises around here. But instead of chastising her, I nodded for her to continue her story. The stern talking-to would come after this mess was over.

"Anyway, I figured the most likely place he'd keep it was his garage in Christmas. It's a legitimate business and, as far as I know, not connected to any of Jose's illegal stuff."

This part, I suspected, was a lie. A careful ruse to keep Ursula from knowing the truth about the magical charm she'd used to track the bag down.

"So, I go there, sneak inside, and..."

"Wait a minute." Ever the lawyer, Ursula's ears had perked up a bit. "When you say 'sneak inside,' what you're really saying is..."

Trixie nodded, her cheeks blushing yet again. "I broke in. Yeah. But it was for a good cause!"

"Honey, I thought we'd talked about this," Ursula said. "There's never a good reason to break the law. You have your future to think about. You lucked out with Tom here, but other business owners wouldn't have taken you in and given you a job. Most of them would press charges and hope they never see you again."

"But...I..."

"I'm serious." Ursula was in no mood for Trixie's back talk. "With your rap sheet, any new offenses on your record could cause repercussions that—"

"Ursula!" I snapped. "Enough! Let the girl finish her story. I'll talk to her later about all this."

The attorney's eyes narrowed at me, and I immediately regretted barking at her like I had, but I also didn't like her grilling the poor girl when she'd been so proud of discovering the mobster's property.

I motioned for Trixie to continue. She smiled at me with a nod of thanks and proceeded with her tale.

"Anyway, once I was inside, it didn't take me long to find the bag. That idiot Jose didn't even bother putting it in his safe. Just put it in one of the drawers in a file cabinet. He locked it, but a simple paperclip opened it right up. Once I found the bag, I hightailed it back here."

Leopards and their spots. I truly believed they could change, but it took lots of time and infinite amounts of patience. Trixie had been a thief most of her life. It's all she really knew until she met me and became part of my life, my mission, and this House. I couldn't expect her to simply forget all the things she used to do so well just because she had turned so much of her life around.

And although I would never admit it to Ursula, I couldn't have been more proud of her. Oh, the responsible part of me still intended to have a good long talk with her later, but at that moment, I practically swelled with pride.

21

So, you have it?" Vinnie Tarturo asked. He took hold of the back of the kitchen chair, as if afraid it might fly away, and carefully sat down. Jimmy and Louis once again stood behind him. They seemed even more wary than they'd been yesterday.

I took the seat opposite their boss.

"First of all, you should know," I began, "it was never in my shop. We found it somewhere else." I paused for effect. "*With* someone else."

I wasn't entirely sure I wanted to play this game with the gangster, but I was curious as to his reaction, which was simply one raised eyebrow and, "Really?"

I nodded.

"Care to tell me who had it?"

I shook my head. "Nope. It's not my job to help you carry out vendettas in Christmas."

Tarturo chuckled. "I got ways of gettin' it out of you, ya know."

"Not in *this* House, you don't."

In response to my words, the foundation of the old place gave a quiet shudder. The goons and their boss's eyes all darted this way and that, and I smiled at their discomfort. I looked over at Louis. "Tinsel's been asking about you," I lied. "You remember Tinsel, right? My guard alligator?" The big guy's eyes widened, his complexion turning nearly the color of the snow outside at the mention of the gator. "Seems he hasn't eaten in a while, and you looked like more than a morsel for him."

I knew I really shouldn't be poking the mafioso bear. I'd most likely pay for it later. But right now, it was too much fun.

"The money, Mr. Nast," Tarturo interrupted my fun and games. "If you please."

"And you'll leave us alone?"

He offered a single nod. "You have my solemn word."

I wasn't sure what his word was worth; but I figured, for now, I had little choice in the matter. I stood and walked over to the kitchen cabinets. I knew Peppermint was somewhere in the kitchen, watching my back, so I wasn't too concerned about their seeing where I'd stashed the duffel and shooting me in the back where I stood. Still, my legs were wobbling underneath me when I crouched and opened the cabinet door under the kitchen sink before pulling the bag out. I walked it back over to the table and set it down for Tarturo to examine.

"Fifty grand, just like you said," I told him, omitting the fact that I'd removed another fifty thousand. I wasn't sure who the other half of the loot belonged to, but I wasn't going to let it out of my sight until I knew for sure. Last thing I needed was another gangster knocking on my door and threatening those I loved.

Tarturo efficiently shuffled the cash, doing mental calculations in his head. "This is all you found?"

"Why?" I asked. "Was there something else Hank took from you?"

The corner of his mouth curled up on one side, and he zipped up the bag. Before he could take it and stand, my hand slapped down on top of the bag. "One question before you go."

He arched an irritated eyebrow at me.

"Indulge me," I said. "A man was murdered in my store. I need to know if it was connected to that money."

He glanced over at his goons, then nodded at me to proceed.

"That money," I said. "It's the exact amount you took from George Trabor and Teddy Gorshon. Their portion of the investment Hank brokered with you."

"I ain't hearin' a question."

"Am I right?"

His eyes drifted up to the ceiling for a moment, then he gave me a slow nod.

"So, here's my real question. Hank was trying to turn over a new leaf. He wasn't happy with how you screwed over his old friends, so he took the money back. Right?"

Vinnie chuckled, but there was no humor in it. In fact, if a shark could laugh, I imagined it would sound something like what he did in my kitchen. "Your deductive skills are impeccable," he finally said. "However, if you think I scammed them out of this money, you'd be mistaken. They signed contracts. Everything was aboveboard. The money, whatever Mr. Trabor and Mr. Gorshon claim, is legally mine. And I certainly wouldn't kill to get back such a paltry sum."

It was my turn to smile. Whether I wanted to admit it or not, I no longer considered Vinnie Tarturo a suspect. He spoke of Teddy in the present tense. He had no idea the man was dead, and I was almost certain *his* killer had murdered Hank as well. "You might not kill to get it back, but you certainly had no qualms about threatening a defenseless twenty-one-year-old girl."

I rose to my feet and glared down at him. The House began to rumble under my feet. Louis let out a low moan at the sensation. For his part, Vinnie merely matched my glare.

"Mr. Nast," he said, getting to his feet, straightening his tie, and slipping on his long wool coat. "It was a pleasure doin' business with ya." He pulled the duffel bag from the table, and it slapped against his thigh with a heavy thud. "Have a very merry Christmas, would ya?"

With that, he nodded to his boys, and the trio stalked out of my kitchen, allowing me a few moments for my muscles to ease out of the tense coils they'd bunched into during the encounter. I let out a deep breath, thankful that that part of my day was finally out of the way.

It was a toss-up between visiting Jose Jimenez or finally getting around to visiting Mallory O'Hare to confront her about what I'd learned from George Trabor a couple of days earlier. Ever since Trixie had discovered Vinnie Tarturo's bag in the mechanic's garage, he'd moved to the top of my suspect list. Whether or not Trixie was right about Hank not returning to pick up the bag after their fight, if Jose had seen Hank with the bag and suspected what was inside, it took very little imagination to believe he might follow the man in the soiled Santa suit to my shop and kill him for it.

Granted, it didn't explain the custom pocketknife being used as the murder weapon, but I suppose Hank could still have had it after all these years. From my investigation, it was beginning to sound as if Hank really *had* been trying to change his ways. If that was the case, a memento such as that knife might have acted as an anchor to the man he wanted to become again.

Despite the knife, Jose was a good suspect, in my opinion. I remembered how elusive he'd been when I'd questioned him at Stuart's Pub. How, after asking him why his shop had been closed on a weekday, his overly large companions had tossed me out. Suspect or not, the man had something to hide. I finally decided that my first stop, after renting a car, would be his garage.

When I pulled into the parking lot of Jimenez Foreign and Domestic Repair, the parking lot was empty. The garage doors were pulled down and locked with deadbolts. No one answered the knocks I made on the office door. Peering through the windows built into the garage doors, I couldn't see so much as a wrench or a screwdriver.

By all accounts, the place looked abandoned. Cleaned out. Jimenez had apparently flown the coop.

"Well," I said to myself, sliding back into the driver's seat of the rental. "Guess it's a Mallory visit after all."

I pulled out of the lot and turned on to County Road 304, navigating the snowswept streets toward the O'Hare estate. I knew she wasn't going to be happy to see me; but then, after what I'd learned about her and her relationship with Trixie and her mother, I didn't care. The old bat had a lot of explaining to do, and I intended for her to tell me everything she knew about Cobb's murder.

As I drove, I thought back to the gunman at Teddy Gorshon's place last night. The high-pitched cry that came when my flashlight had struck the hand holding the gun. It was certainly plausible that a man could emit such a yell; but Occam's razor, which suggests that the simplest solution is most often the correct one, would say that the suspect could, in fact, be a woman. At least, the suspect that had tried to kill me last night, that is. There was no guarantee that that person and Cobb's killer were one and the same, though I was willing to gamble on the chance that they were.

22

I f I'd been sweating over the ordeal that I'd endured earlier with mobster Vinnie Tarturo, I was practically Niagara Falls by the time I drove the rental car up the long winding drive-way of Mallory O'Hare's sprawling estate. The snowstorm, surprisingly, had devolved into sporadic flurries, and the temperature had climbed to an almost-balmy thirty-one degrees. And yet, despite the chill air, my cheeks and ears burned with a heat that can only come from intense stress and worry.

Mallory would not be pleased to see me, I knew. Even less so when she discovered the purpose of my uninvited visit. But if I was going to see this investigation through, it was a necessary evil that I couldn't put off any longer.

I won't lie to you and say that there wasn't a part of me—the not-so-Santa part of me—that rather hoped the spinster heiress to the O'Hare fortune would indeed turn out to be the killer. I'm not proud of it, but it's the truth nonetheless. She was a miserable woman who could only find an ounce of happiness by making those around her miserable as well. For years, I had tried every trick in the book to break down her iron walls and reach the young girl I thought lurked somewhere in her withered soul. And each time I had tried, she'd volleyed back with an attack on my business or those I cared about.

The mansion that Mallory called home was a luxurious an-tebellum affair that had once been the epicenter of a thriving cotton plantation. Its façade, perfectly whitewashed, came complete with seven enormous Corinthian columns that held up the roof covering the immense wraparound front porch, where two massive oak doors led into the home's interior.

Although there was a doorbell mounted to the right of the door, I opted to use the heavy brass knocker instead—partially because I knew how annoying it was for the old hag. I gave it four loud taps and then stepped back to greet whoever was about to answer the door.

I waited a few moments with no answer, then rapped on the door again. Soon, it swung inward to reveal a severe-looking gentleman in a three-piece suit. He was balding, with salt-and-pepper hair encircling his skull, and sporting a pencil moustache that would have made Clark Gable green with envy. He was tall, only a few inches shorter than myself, with the straight-edged posture of a consummate manservant.

"Yes?" he said. "May I help you?"

He had no discernible accent, but his voice oozed with disdain, as if my very presence carried with it a foul stench. Granted, I hadn't had time to shower that day, but I was pretty sure I didn't smell *that* bad.

Cinnamon and gingerbread. That's what Trixie always told me was my natural scent, for some reason.

"Um, yeah. I'm Thomas Nast. I'm hoping I can speak with Ms. O'Hare for a few minutes."

He gazed disapprovingly as he took in my colorful red business suit with silk green vest, green bow tie, and bowler hat, then he sniffed. "You may wait in the foyer while I see if the missus is seeing visitors today." He gestured inside. "Just a moment, please."

He moved like a skeletal marionette through the marble-tiled room, past the large, curved staircase, and toward the back of the house. When he'd disappeared, I took a few minutes to appreciate the house's regal décor. Original oil paintings lined the wall to my left, many from artists I'd seen in museums around the world. A bust of Johnson O'Hare, Mallory's grandfather, sat on a marble pedestal to my right. The place seemed as crisp and cold as a mausoleum, with not even a dash of holly, mistletoe, or Christmas lights to commemorate the splendid holiday that was only a few days away.

I shuddered to think that, if she had her way, the entire town of Christmas—or maybe O'Hareville or whatever she wanted to call it—the place I'd called home for so many years, would become as desolate and joyless as the stone-cold foyer I was now standing in.

Soon, Mallory's butler—he'd never offered his name, and I'll admit I'd been too intimidated to ask—returned to usher me through the maze of hallways that eventually led into the mansion's parlor. There, reclining on a divan with a martini in her hand, was Mallory O'Hare, shredding me to pieces with her razor's-edge glare.

"Mr. Nast, just a moment," she said, raising a hand to stop me from speaking. "August, have you seen the boy today?"

"No, madam," the butler, apparently named August, said. "He's not been in the yard all day."

The yard. I guessed she was referring to Eli.

"Well, he has the work truck," she said. "When he returns, be sure he's taken the time to wash it and refill the gas tank, or take it out of his pay. We're not going to keep funding his excursions into town. Am I clear?"

"Crystal, ma'am."

With that, the butler turned and walked out of the parlor, closing the door behind him.

Finally, the old crone graced me with a glance in my direction. "So, Mr. Nast, what can I do for you on this unusually cold day?"

At the mention of the weather, I stifled an impulse to remind her that she should feel right at home in the freezing temperatures. But wisdom won out in the end. It wouldn't do to make the already-hostile woman even more so before I'd had a chance to ask my questions.

I took a seat on an Edwardian-era sofa opposite my host and gave her my most ingratiating smile. It was a difficult challenge as I gazed at the wrinkled, sourfaced husk of a woman sitting across from me. She was small in stature. Thin, but not healthy-looking. Her brown shoulder-length hair—obviously heavily dyed—was straight and rigid, though I expected there wouldn't have been a split end among the lot. Her gaunt face was lathered in a full palette of rich red lipstick that served only to emphasize a gash of a mouth, sky-blue eyeliner, and dark tan blush that treated her wrinkled old visage more like a canvas of expressionist art than a face. Then there was her nose. Overly large and bulbous, with the protruding veins that only come with years of excessive drinking. In short, her physical appearance perfectly matched the withering soul within.

Then again, I could be biased: I just really didn't like this woman.

"I haven't got all day, Mr. Nast. Get to the point of your visit, or please see yourself out."

I suppressed an urge to cough, finding my throat suddenly of the consistency of sandpaper. My tongue clung to the roof of my mouth as I struggled to find the best way to approach the reason for my visit.

"Sorry to bother you, Ms. Mallory." Everyone in Christmas

referred to her that way. She insisted that the use of her surname made her feel old. "Um, let me get to the point."

"That would be a novelty." She sipped at her martini with a wry smile and, for the first time, I noticed the elastic bandage wrapped around her bony wrist. My heart quickened at the sight. I'd injured the hand of my attacker last night with my flashlight. Could it have been Mallory after all? Did I dare hope?

I shook the thought away and decided to stick to the script I'd concocted while driving here. I couldn't let myself get distracted. "Yeah, well, I'm sure, by now, you've heard about the murder of Hank Cobb."

She sneered at this, turning up her nose at the mention of the man's name. "Just one less dreg I'll have to deal with once we're incorporated." She paused, giving me a serpentine grin. "I guess that's one down, a few more undesirables to go."

I wanted to ask the old crone what I had ever done to her to make her so hostile toward me and my store, but there was no point. We'd had that conversation on more than one occasion in the past, and it never went anywhere. She'd never liked Horatio either, but I think that had more to do with unrequited love than anything else. She'd always had not-so-secret intentions for my old mentor.

"Good for you," I told her. "I'm glad Cobb's death pleases you. But I can assure you, Ms. Mallory, I don't intend to make it so easy when it's my time."

"Mr. Nast, get on with it or I'll have August toss you out on that bony rear of yours."

"Fine. Since you brought up how much Hank Cobb's death benefits you, I'll just come out and ask. Did you kill him, you ol' harpy?"

I realize that the "harpy" thing was unnecessarily combative, but she was intentionally pushing my buttons. I'm only human. For now.

Her brows furrowed, knitting at the top of her nose into an ugly patchwork of angry wrinkles. Her eyes seemed to boil inside her skull as she glared at me.

"How dare you." The words were a deep-throated whisper, making them sound far more dangerous than if she'd shouted them from the top of her mansion.

"Well, sorry. It just seems like you're a little too excited over the murder." I pointed to her injured wrist. "Then there's that. Someone killed Teddy Gorshon last night and tried to kill me too. They fled the scene, I'm pretty sure, with a major booboo on their hand or arm." I leaned forward on the sofa, my rear on the very edge of the cushion. "I'm curious about how you happened to hurt yours."

Her brows twisted nearly into knots as she took another sip from her martini glass, and she shrugged. "Not that it's any of your business," she said. Each syllable sounded like it was spiked with cobra venom. "I'm an old woman. Fragile bones. And I have the tendency to fall from time to time."

I could understand that. The woman's liver must be pickled by now with all the booze she consumed. I'm sure that made her pretty unsteady on her feet.

"This happened two nights ago." She shifted her glass from one hand to the other and held up her injured one. "While getting out of bed in the middle of the night. Would you like a doctor's note? X-rays, maybe? How about a notarized affidavit from August?"

I rolled my eyes at her sarcasm, then waved her protests away. There was no way to know if she was really telling the truth or not, and I chided myself for getting sidetracked despite my best efforts not to. I decided to return to my original line of questioning.

"Fine. But back to Hank's murder, I *did* hear that the two of you were arguing—probably in this very room—the day before he was killed."

I didn't have to worry about poor Eli getting in trouble for ratting the old woman out. The O'Hare estate was the largest employer in town, with literally dozens of people coming and going from the house daily. She'd have no idea who'd passed the juicy bit of gossip on to me, and I wasn't about to tell her.

She continued to stare at me, her lower jaw moving from side to side, like a cow chewing on a hunk of cud. The wrinkles around her lips—the telltale sign of a lifelong smoker—writhed about, like some ritualistic death-curse dance by an irate shaman. I'm not sure I'd ever seen her this angry before, and I'll admit to maybe enjoying it just a tad too much.

After another moment, I cocked my head to one side. "Well, Ms. Mallory? Mind telling me what you two argued about?"

"As a matter of fact, I do. I don't see that it's any of *your* business."

I paused, contemplating my approach here. In the end, I decided honesty was probably the best way to go.

"You're right. It's not."

She looked at me, her eyes narrowing as if trying to decipher whether I was playing a game or not.

"I'm serious. It's none of my business." I leaned back in the sofa in a relaxed pose, one knee crossing the other and an arm draped casually over the top of the seat. "But Trixie's being accused of the murder, so I'm *making* it my business."

She blinked at this. The woman seemed genuinely stunned.

"Tricia...I mean, Ms. McNamara?" she said. "She's being accused of killing her..." She seemed to nearly choke upon speaking the next word, which kind of threw me a bit. "...father?"

I nodded. "She's the Sheriff's Office's prime suspect, I'd say. No formal charges, and her attorney assured me the evidence is circumstantial at best. But still. I don't want her to go through this. I'll do whatever is necessary to see to it that she doesn't."

"You truly care for that little delinquent with her burgundy lipstick and dog collars, don't you?" There was a twinkle in the old bag's eyes. She seemed to have recovered from her momentary lapse of sympathy and returned to her cold-blooded venom. "Good. You two deserve each other. That girl's caused as much trouble around here as her father. With her gone to prison, it'll be easier to evict you from that firetrap of a house of yours."

My mouth dropped. I couldn't believe what I was hearing. I knew O'Hare was vindictive and power-hungry, but I never imagined her to be this heartless. This sociopathic. Especially when it came to her own granddaughter. I was pretty sure her response was an act to throw me off balance. After all, she didn't know that I already knew—or guessed—the nature of hers and Hank's argument. Maybe it was time that I dropped that little bombshell in her lap.

I stood up to my full six-foot-eight-inch height and loomed over her as she sat coolly on her divan.

"I'm surprised at you, Ms. Mallory," I told her, "talking about your own flesh and blood like that. Your grandkid, no less."

She gasped. Her eyes widened so much, it threatened to smooth out all the wrinkles from her face.

"How did..." She fumbled to bring her glass to her lips before taking a long gulp from it. "How did you know?"

I shrugged. "Turns out I'm a much better detective than I

thought. I also know that's the reason for your argument with Hank. He threatened to tell the world about your little secret, didn't he?"

She laughed behind dead eyes. "He's been threatening that for years. Ever since he found out about Ellie, he's been blackmailing me every month. Not much, mind you. But enough."

I nodded. "But this time he wanted more, right? A considerable bit more. Maybe enough to kill him over?"

"Please." She waved the accusation away with a flick of her uninjured wrist. "It would take a lot more money than that to sully my hands on the likes of him." Mallory leaned back on the divan, her eyes drifting up to the high vaulted ceiling as if in thought. "But that's not what he wanted at all. He didn't want my money. He told me he wanted to turn his life around. Wanted to reconnect with Tricia. Start over with her. He planned on taking her away from here. Away from Christmas!"

My jaw nearly dropped at the implication of what she was saying.

"Away from you?"

She stared at me for a moment, and I watched as her chiseled cadaverous features softened. A gleam formed in the corner of one eye.

"Yes, if you must know," she said before taking another sip of the martini. "I had never done right by her mother, as you obviously already know. Ellie was a source of great embarrassment to me during a simpler time. But Tricia? I've watched her grow up in Christmas. Watched her in her worst and in her best. When possible, I've helped her secretly here and there."

"The scholarship," I muttered. "The scholarship she didn't even apply for that lets her go to college."

She nodded. "Truth is, Mr. Nast, there isn't much in my life with any sort of emotional connection. For the most part, I prefer it that way. But watching Tricia from afar has helped, somewhat, to feel part of something other than my own ambitions."

I stood there, stunned. Unable to find any words that might defuse the tension I was currently feeling.

"Hank Cobb wanted to take Tricia away from me," she continued. "I couldn't allow that."

My heart thudded against my chest. Was she about to confess to his murder?

"So, I did what I've been doing all along," she said. "I paid him. Paid him more money than he ever imagined. Fifty thousand dollars. To leave Christmas—and Tricia—and never look back."

Okay. So, not a confession. But at least the mystery of the extra money in the duffel had been solved. Yet, still...

"But Hank decided to go back on his deal with you," I told her. "He approached Trixie the night he died. Pleaded with her to come with him. Swore he had changed." I dug my hands in my trouser pockets and leaned toward her. "I wonder what you might have done if you'd found out about that."

It was her turn to stand from the couch. Slowly. A little unsteadily. But she lifted herself to her feet, looked up into my eyes. She only came up to the lower portion of my chest; but even with her frail frame and unsteady gait, she was still far more intimidating than I could ever hope to be.

"I would have paid him five hundred thousand more." Her voice was ice-cold. Gone was the echo of humanity I'd heard when she talked about the joy she'd had watching Trixie grow up. In its place was the purr of the feline predator. "I would have paid him a million. It honestly didn't matter to me, Mr. Nast. Whether he had really changed or was simply playing another con, Hank Cobb had his price. I didn't need to kill him. It was only a matter of time before I found what that price was."

She strode over to the wet bar and poured herself another drink. After taking a sip, she laughed. "You know, I'm rather surprised that you're having such trouble solving this little mystery. There can be no shortage of suspects. The vile man was loathed by so many in this town." She turned to look at me, a sinister smile spread across her haggard face. "The way the Smart boy tells it, you're the *real* Santa Claus." She laughed again. It reminded me of the sound of crows cawing over the remains of a decomposing body. "He says you have magic powers. Real magic! So, let me ask you, Santa Man, why don't you use some of those magic powers to figure out who the real killer is and leave me alone."

Without any warning, she hurled her glass in my direction. As I ducked, it sailed past my head and shattered on the stone fireplace behind me. Out of further danger, I stood to my full height and began walking toward the parlor door.

"Fine," I said. "I'll leave. But rest assured, if I find out you are responsible for Hank's death in any way, I'll be out front when the police come to your house to put the cuffs on you. Trust me on that."

She laughed again, pouring another drink, then wobbled back to the divan. "Trust me," she said. "I have nothing to fear from you. And you're wrong. It'll be me standing outside that tourist trap of *yours* when the police come to place the eviction notice in your hands."

The two of us stared each other down for several uncomfortable moments before Mallory O'Hare picked up a bell from an end table next to the divan and gave it a jingle. Within seconds, the butler strode into the room.

"August," she said, "show Mr. Nast to the door, please; and afterward, please ring up the police. I'd like to report his harassment personally to the detective in charge of Hank Cobb's murder investigation."

I held my ground, my heart hammering against my chest. I was furious, but I knew there was nothing I could do about it. Whether she'd killed Hank or not, there was nothing more I was going to learn from her, and from this point forward, I was trespassing on her property. Tice was going to have a field day with my coming here to interview the crone. To level more accusations would only land me in jail, and I wouldn't do Trix much good like that. After taking a deep breath, I turned to leave.

"Oh, Mr. Nast?"

I turned around to face her.

"I should warn you that sharing what you've learned about me with my granddaughter would be slander at best. Without proof. If you so much as breathe a word that I'm her grandmother— and she's my heir—I'll see you in court faster than reindeer on Christmas Eve."

With a nod to the butler, I was ushered out of the parlor and out the door of the most opulent mansion in Central Florida.

23

My mind raced on my drive back to Wonderland. Something Mallory had said in our conversation had unsettled me, but I couldn't quite place what it was. A small factoid. Something seemingly insignificant, but profound at the same time. What was it?

I white-knuckled the steering wheel as I rounded a curve along County Road 304, heading back into town. The snow had once again picked up, and as the setting sun glared through my windshield, the entire world seemed sheathed in a Creamsicle blanket of blinding orange light.

The dangerous driving conditions set my thoughts along a tangent path. I would not want to meet a drunk driver along this road right now. In fact, as bright as the sunset glare was on the falling snow, I was hoping not to meet any other traffic at all along the way. But the thought made me wonder. How many of my suspects—how many people in Christmas, really—suffered from alcoholism? It all started with that random AA token I'd found under the sofa the day I discovered Hank's body. Since then, I'd seemed to run into so many people suffering from the condit—

My scrambling thoughts came to a screeching halt. I suddenly slammed on my brakes and skidded a few yards until my rental car did the same. My pulse raced. My heart threatened to clamber up my throat and run for cover at the idea I was now formulating about the murder.

No. It couldn't be... No. No. No. But...

After a few minutes to calm my nerves, I resumed my drive back to Wonderland. By the time I turned from 304 onto Cupid Avenue, I was doing several mental calculations regarding the Christmas knives. Who of my suspects were still missing their pocketknives? George had his. So did Teddy, although his death pretty much eliminated him as a suspect. Bill Sweeney had his all nice and displayed in a custom shadow box in his study.

I thought about it some more. They were all accounted for, right?

No. Alphonso Garcia had lost his in the move to their home a few years back. And what about Hank's? I had given Hank a knife too. Trixie didn't know where it was, or if her father had even kept it after all these years. But it was still unaccounted for. For all I knew, he'd pawned it for beer money at some point. Anyone in Christmas could have that knife.

I wasn't liking where my mind was taking me, and I was trying everything I could to find a different solution. Doing anything I could think of in hopes of a better suspect.

Skidding into Wonderland's empty parking lot, I leaped from the car and half-scrambled, half-skated my way to the porch steps and through the front doors. The store had closed about thirty minutes earlier, so I knew my crew and I would be safe to talk about my theory.

No, Nast. You've got to be wrong about this.

But it all made so much sense. Everything.

No. No. No. Don't even think about it. You've got to be wrong!

"Trixie? Peppermint? You here?" I shouted.

If it hadn't been that one thing Mallory had said—and something that Ursula had told me the night before—I wouldn't be struggling with this gut-wrenching realization.

Dang them both.

"Trixie?"

"Sheesh, Beanpole, knock it off. Some of us are trying to relax after a long day of humans mucking about the place with all their Christmas cheer."

I wheeled around at the disembodied voice. "Pep? Where's Trix?"

"Where do you think? She left five minutes after the store closed."

"She's with Seth?"

"Duh, you dum-dum."

The House grumbled under our feet.

I spun around, trying to locate the little imp. "Pep, where are you?"

"Right here."

I turned again. "Stop moving. I need to focus on you." I looked up into the vaulted ceiling. "House, make the lights right."

Instantly, the lights around the myriad of Christmas-tree displays dimmed. The overhead fluorescents shut off completely. A couple of spotlights from the second-floor landing shifted to hues of red and green and swiveled in our direction, landing on a single spot on the floor just a couple of feet in front of me. Slowly, a figure began to materialize. The generalized shape of a diminutive man. For a moment, I caught the impression of buckskin and a bear pelt. A few feathers hanging from where the figure's head was—the telltale sign of a creature of Seminole legend. The clothing, however, shifted quickly to a red-and-green pinstriped suit and bowler hat, mimicking my own attire. Soon I got the best vision of the elf I was likely to get on this side of Wyndter.

"What is it, boss?" Peppermint asked. "You're starting to concern me."

I crouched down to look the little guy in the eye. "You *should* be concerned," I told him. "I believe every second Trixie is with Seth Timmons is a second she's in horrible danger."

I heard the elf inhale, but I held up a finger to stop him. "Peppermint, I know you love that girl every bit as much as I do. Because of that, I'm about to do something I never thought I would. I'm going to release you—temporarily—from the bond of the House. I need you to find Trixie and keep her safe while I double-check a few things. I'm also going to call Ursula and ask her to head over to Seth's place. Nothing should happen to Trix if people are around. She should be safe, as long as you get to her ASAP."

"You're serious? You're letting me out?"

I wanted to smile at Peppermint's obvious excitement over the prospect of being able to leave the premises for the first time in over a hundred years, but the situation was too dire. I couldn't enjoy the moment as much as I would have liked.

In answer to his question, I stood to my full height and looked down at the elf while taking a deep breath.

"Minlytryasan, of the *este lopocke* people, I give you permission to leave this House for the sole purpose of protecting Tricia 'Trixie' McNamara from *bodily* harm." I stressed the word "bodily" to rein him in from messing with Seth for other issues. "The moment your task is over, you will be compelled to return and once again be subject to the laws imposed on you by your former master, Horatio Longpepper."

There was a moment of silence; then the elf looked up at me with a grin. "Done. And done."

With that, he popped out of existence, leaving me alone to consider my next move.

❄

It was nearly eleven thirty by the time I pulled into the parking lot of Seth Timmons's apartment complex. It had been nearly four and a half hours since I released Peppermint, but the world hadn't ended in a fiery explosion, and Trixie—according to my last conversation with Ursula on the phone—was still very much alive and safe. So, despite the horrific pit I had roiling in my stomach over what was about to happen, I considered it a win.

By the time I got out of my rental car, Ursula, Trixie, and a half-baked Seth Timmons scurried out of his apartment and meandered over to me with quizzical expressions on their faces.

"Tom, care to explain what's going on?" Trixie asked, shivering beneath the hoodie she was wearing. Floridians, who have no need for winter clothes for the most part, are never prepared for cold weather.

I glanced around the parking lot, making sure we were alone. Besides the pelting of ice crystals falling against the metal roofs of the various cars in the parking lot, there didn't appear to be any movement at all.

"Let's go inside, and I'll explain everything." I took hold of her elbow and nudged her in the direction of the building.

She shrugged away and looked up at me defiantly. "If this is another one of your 'I don't trust Seth' things, you and I are going to have problems."

"It's not. I promise." Once again, I took her elbow.

"Tom," I heard Peppermint whisper near my ear. "I think we've got compan—"

Before he could finish the warning, a shot rang out, echoing throughout the complex. Something slammed into the back window of my rental, shattering the glass in a spiderweb of shards. Instantly, we all dropped to the ground. I covered Trixie's body with my own as more shots were fired from an unknown location.

"Pep? You got eyes on him?" I asked the thin air around me.

"I saw a glint of metal just before the gunshot," the elf told me. "But now I've lost it."

"What's happening?" Seth shouted. His hands were covering his ears and he writhed on the ground in a panic. I watched as Ursula scrambled over to him and placed her arm around his shoulder. "Someone's shooting at me! They're shooting at me!"

I heard the elf growl with irritation, but I snapped my fingers to grab his attention. "Scout ahead, Pep. See if you can find him."

"Aye, aye."

Another shot echoed in the distance. Something pounded the pavement near my rear tires, sending a wave of asphalt shrapnel our way. Considering that all the gunshots had landed around my vicinity, I figured the killer was once again targeting me, despite the fact that Trixie was safely underneath my prone form.

Risking a glance up, I scanned the parking lot. As I did, I caught sight of a figure dashing from the shadows of one live oak tree to another, then straight over a bluff, and out of sight. A moment later, I heard the sound of an engine revving, followed by the squeal of tires in the distance.

"He's gone," Peppermint said near my ear.

"Did you get a good look at him?"

There was silence.

"You know I can't see you shake your head, right?"

"Oh, right," Pep said. "No. Unfortunately, he had hopped in a pickup truck and was gone before I had a good bead on him."

I sighed. "It doesn't matter," I told him. "I already know who it was."

24

Detective Tice grumbled incessantly when I refused to tell him my theory about the killer, instead insisting that all the suspects meet at Wonderland the next morning for a final confrontation. Maybe I'd read one too many Agatha Christie stories, but after the crap the homicide detectives had put Trixie and me through for the past week, I had decided that they owed it to us to let me do things my way. In the end, it had been Detective Lassiter who had convinced her partner that it would be easier to comply with my ridiculous demands.

A "Sorry, We're Closed" sign now hung on the front door of the shop, and I watched as Alphonso Garcia and his wife—the last two people to show up—were led to their assigned seats in the center of the showroom floor.

I stood over by the cash register, looking at the assembled group. George and Margaret Trabor sat next to each other on the side closest to the front door, where two uniformed deputies stood guard. Pastor Bill Sweeney and his wife were next, then Al and Cindy. I couldn't help the grin that spread across my face as Vinnie Tarturo and his two shadows hunkered nervously in chairs on the far side of the showroom. Vinnie's eyes shot daggers at me under hooded brows. Trixie, Seth, Ursula, and Eli Smart hung out behind the counter with me.

Only two people were unaccounted for among the possible suspects in Hank Cobb's death: Mallory O'Hare and Jose

Jimenez. Truth be told, I had a feeling that Jose would never be found. Something told me that Vinnie and his goons had figured out where we'd found his money and had taken care of the mechanic once and for all. I had no proof of that, mind you; but since the police had been unable to locate him, it was just my gut feeling. Which was fine, because I didn't think he'd been the one to kill Hank anyway.

As for Mallory, I hadn't expected her to accept my invitation to this little party, which was okay as well. She might be an evil harpy-like Scrooge of a woman, but I was pretty confident she wasn't the murderer either. Like she had said, if she'd wanted to deal with Hank, it wouldn't have been too difficult to discover his price. Despite that, I'd sent her a private letter, delivered earlier that morning by Tice, for clarification on a single issue. She'd responded in kind, but with another warning to keep her family secret to myself. Or else.

"All right, Nast," Detective Tice growled as he stepped over to the central Christmas tree—the same tree I'd found Hank's body under—and addressed the room. "Enough of the theatrics. How about you tell us what this is all about?"

Taking my cane, I moved around the counter and approached him, taking a long look at the crowd with a confident smile plastered on my face. A smile I didn't feel. It was more for the detectives' sakes than mine or my guests'. I needed them to understand that I had everything under control, although I hated myself for what I was about to do.

"Good morning, everyone," I said, sidling up to the brutish detective and offering a nod to each of my guests. "Thank you for coming today."

"Ain't like we had much choice, now, did we?" Vinnie Tarturo spat, glaring at the deputies guarding the front door.

I waved his comment away. "I figure you all know why you're here."

"I assume you have new information about Hank's and Teddy's deaths," Al Garcia said.

"Were they connected, ya think?" asked Pastor Bill.

"They had to be," George Trabor added. "Two murders in Christmas, so close together? That can't be a coincidence."

I watched Margaret nudge her husband before shushing him. "Let Tom get on with it, George. The suspense is killing me."

"It's killing me too," Detective Tice said with a snarl. "I warned you about playing detective, Nast. If you don't produce the killer, along with motive and some good evidence, I've got a good mind to take you in and charge you with hindering a police investigation."

I nodded, indicating that I understood. "You all are correct," I began. "I think I know who the killer is." I looked over at my old friend George and gave him a thumbs-up. "And you're right. Teddy's and Hank's murders are connected. However, Teddy's death was for the simplest of reasons. Self-preservation. You see, Teddy had somehow figured out who the killer was. He was going to tell me, but was killed before he could."

"So, who did it?" Eli said, looking around the room at all the suspects. His hands stuffed into his pants pockets, he practically shuddered with anticipation.

I held up a finger. "Before I do, I need to go through all the facts. First of all, I don't think Hank was the primary target in this thing."

"Huh?" Tice asked. "It's kind of hard to murder someone with a pocketknife accidentally. Seems to me, the killer definitely wanted Cobb dead."

"Oh, he did. Definitely. But his murder was a means to an

end and nothing more." I began pacing the floor. As I did, I looked past the uniformed deputies at the door and watched as the deadbolt turned by its own volition. We were now all safely secure inside the House. "You see, I was the intended target all along."

"You?" Trixie asked. "How?"

"The killer is angry with me. He blames me for something terrible that happened to him. Something he thinks I could have prevented but didn't."

"Well, that leaves me out," Vinnie Tarturo said. "I'd never even met ya until the other day."

"That doesn't necessarily mean you're innocent, Vinnie." I threw him a knowing wink. "I'm sure these nice detectives would love to talk to you about Jose Jimenez later." He stiffened at the mention of the mechanic's name. "But for now, back to our killer. With Hank's death, he was trying to figuratively kill two birds with one stone: get rid of a major roadblock in something he desperately desired, while also framing me for the murder."

"But I was the police's prime suspect from day one," Trixie said. "That doesn't make sense."

"That's because the killer had no idea about the argument you had with Hank at Stuart's the night he was killed. The killer didn't know you had come to Wonderland to sleep off a bender. And he definitely didn't know that Jose Jimenez would have called the police about the altercation in order to steal Vinnie Tarturo's money."

"Okay, Mr. Nast, we've been indulging you as you requested," Detective Lassiter said, stepping up to her partner. "All this is brilliant speculation. But what about the facts?"

"I'm glad you asked, Detective," I said, reaching my hand in my coat pocket and willing the AA token to appear. As it did, I pulled it out and held it up for all to see. "Exhibit A. A simple Alcoholics Anonymous chip. I found it under that sofa after the police left with Hank's body."

"But Janet told you, those are a dime a dozen," Ursula said. "Anyone could have one of those. Heck, it could have been dropped by any of your customers months ago."

"Ah, yes! Correct," I said, not bothering to explain that nothing could remain on my floors for any length of time without being cleaned by the House. "But it's just one tiny piece of the puzzle. I had a feeling that whoever had killed Hank had dropped it, which meant that the killer had a major drinking problem."

"But Hank himself had a drinking problem," Eli reminded us. "Didn't you say he was trying to get his life back on track? Had started seeking help for his drinking?"

"I did indeed, young man." I beamed at him, getting into the groove. "And apparently, a lot of people in this town suffer from the condition. Teddy, Al...heck, even Ursula's assistant, Janet, is a member of AA. No, the chip itself wasn't enough of a clue, which is why I didn't bother sharing it with you two, detectives."

I pressed on before anyone could object.

"The other, much bigger, clue was the knife that was used to kill Hank. A special custom Swiss Army knife I'd gifted to only six people in the world. Exhibit B, in regard to trying to frame me for the murder, by the way." I spun around, taking in the looks everyone in the room was giving me. "If everyone had their knives, then the police would wonder if there might have been a seventh knife I'd never given anyone. That's what I think the killer was thinking anyway. What he didn't know, however, was that at least one of my friends had lost his knife at some point, making him a suspect as well.

"I tried tracking down the knives. Teddy, George, and Bill all had theirs. Alphonso, however, had lost his, which didn't bode well for him for a while during my investigation."

Al blushed at this, and I watched as Cindy placed a loving arm over his shoulder.

"Fortunately, with a little elbow grease and determination, the three of us tore their place apart last night until we found it." I didn't divulge the use of the divining charm as a means of locating it. "Turns out, it had been in a crease under the cushions on their couch all along." I paused for effect. "Now, I knew without a doubt that there wasn't another knife floating around out there. I'd only made six. All the knives were accounted for except two: Hank's..." I glanced over at Eli. "And your dad's knife, Eli. The one I gave Jonathan."

My gaze drifted to Trixie's, whose eyes suddenly widened. I knew what was happening. It had been planned this way. Peppermint was now telling her to move away from the counter and come to me. She was being told to take Ursula by the hand and bring her along too.

"Last night, I called Detective Lassiter up and asked her for a simple favor," I continued as Trixie inched around the corner of the countertop with Ursula in tow. "Check the property list that came with Hank Cobb to the Medical Examiner's Office. With Hank's desire to return to his old, more positive life, I had a feeling what she'd find; and sure enough, I was right. His knife had been in his Santa suit all along."

Truth was, although I hadn't seen the knife, I had indeed felt its minuscule amount of Christmas magic when I'd found Hank's body. It was that magic that had been bothering me about the grime-covered suit from day one.

Eli looked from me to the detectives to Trixie before

returning to me. "My...my dad's knife? I haven't seen that thing in years. I...I..."

I shook my head as I bit back tears that were forming in the corners of my eyes. "Eli, enough. I know it was you. And I know why."

"Wait. You think I killed Hank?" He let out a high-pitched nervous laugh. "That's crazy. I'd never do something like that!"

I moved closer to the counter space, and Eli backed up a single step as I did. "You're in love with Trixie, Eli. I'd never realized just how much until Ursula pointed it out to me, but you're hopelessly in love with her. You overheard Hank talking to Mallory O'Hare the other day about his desire to take Trix away from here, and you couldn't have that. You couldn't bear the thought of her moving away from you."

He blinked. "That's not true." He looked over at Trixie with pleading eyes. "I'd never hurt your father. I wouldn't!"

"But killing Hank wasn't the only thing you realized you could do. You could finally get even with me. Get even for the death of your father." I nodded at Eli's hands, still tucked securely in his trouser pockets. "Why don't you pull your hands out and let us have a look at them?"

He glanced from me to Trixie, but kept his hands buried deep within the pockets.

"This doesn't make any sense," Tice said. "My investigation shows his dad died of cancer. How can he blame you for that?"

I cocked my head and shrugged at Eli. "Do you want to tell them, or do you want me to?"

He stared at me for a long moment as he bit down on his lower lip. I saw a small trickle of crimson form where his teeth had dug into the flesh of his lip. Then, his fury was unleashed.

"You're Santa Claus!" he shouted at the top of his lungs.

"You're freakin' Santa Claus! If anyone could have cured my dad of cancer, it would have been you. But you wouldn't even admit to me who you were. You kept denying it, over and over again. And the more you denied it, the more Dad wasted away to nothing!"

I glanced over at the detectives. "Jonathan passed away on Christmas Eve three years ago." I returned my attention to Eli, who was slavering at the mouth. His hands, now extracted from his pockets, were curled into whitened fists. His right wrist looked bruised and swollen. "And," I continued, "you forget, Horatio Longpepper died of cancer as well. Six years ago. I loved that man like a father. Do you really think if I'd had the power you think I did, I wouldn't have used it to save him?"

"Wait, this kid thinks you're actually Santa Claus?" Lassiter asked.

"*Actual* Santa Claus? This kid thinks Santa is real?" Tice added. "Is he trying to get an insanity plea going?"

"He *is* the real Santa!" Eli shouted. "Or he will be! This House is magic. I've seen it. There's an elf that lives here. I've seen him too!"

"Oh, geez," Tice muttered under his breath.

Before anyone could think to act, Eli bolted. Knowing he could not get past the officers, he dashed in the opposite direction, toward the kitchen. Before he reached the swinging doors, however, he veered left and up the winding staircase to the second floor.

Where he most definitely wasn't invited.

Tice, Lassiter, and one of the officers took off after him, leaving only one deputy to remain on guard at the front door.

"I don't believe it," George said. "Little Eli Smart? The killer?"

I nodded. "It killed me to do that. I had such high hopes for that boy."

"Shouldn't someone go help the police catch him?" Alphonso Garcia asked. "This is a big place. From experience, I know there's lots of hiding spots everywhere."

I gave him a sad smile. "I don't think we have to worry about that. This place has a way of tripping people up when they get lost in here."

Trixie walked up to me and threw her arms around my neck, giving me a big squeeze. I felt moisture from tears soaking into my jacket as she let out a few choking sobs. After a moment, I patted her on her back, and she released me.

"He killed Teddy too?" George asked. "Really?"

I gave another nod. "In fact, it was Teddy who set me on the right path. When Teddy called me to tell me he'd figured it out, the killer showed up. I overheard Teddy say he hadn't done anything to him. Basically, tried to convince the killer he didn't deserve to die. That set me to thinking that this might all be about vengeance. It's what set my mind in Eli's direction."

"What?" Ursula said. "Just that? Someone blamed you and you automatically went to poor Eli?"

"Actually, it was something you said two nights ago when Eli came over to see how Trixie was doing. You said he hung out for a while, then got in his truck and left."

"Yeah. So?"

"Eli's not allowed to drive. His license is suspended. DUI. He rides a bicycle everywhere. But he needed the truck—a truck he used while working for Mallory O'Hare—and she confirmed as much in this." I held up the letter she'd sent back with Detective Tice. "A beat-up white pickup, in fact. The same kind I saw while I was talking to Teddy at his place a few days ago. The same kind that had driven me off the road. And the same that..." I paused, nearly slipping and using Peppermint's name in my recap, "...a witness saw driving away last night after he shot at us in Seth's parking lot. As for the night Teddy died, Eli used the truck to get from Teddy's place to Wonderland after he tried to kill me. He needed to get here before anyone else. To establish an alibi for himself, I suspect."

"Oh, wow," Ursula said, shaking her head.

Suddenly, an earsplitting shriek erupted from the hall above, followed immediately by several more panicked shouts. Eli Smart raced into view, stumbling down the stairs again at top speed. The detectives and uniformed officer quickly followed. Each of their eyes was stretched beyond credulity.

"It's a gator!" Tice shouted while racing down the steps. "A freakin' alligator!"

I glanced over at Louis and Jimmy sitting on either side of Vinnie Tarturo, smug smiles on their faces.

"There's a freakin' alligator up there!" Tice shouted again as he picked himself up off the floor after tumbling down the last three steps and turned his sidearm in the direction of the second floor.

Eli tried to scramble out of sight before anyone could catch up to him, but a sly whip of my cane brought his feet flying out from under him. He spun his arms wildly before catching his balance. Then he continued his sprint straight for the door until an invisible force seemed to trip him out of the blue and he plowed into an oak coffee table just a few feet away. A moment later, Lassiter was on top of him, placing him in handcuffs.

"Thanks for the assist," I mumbled out of the corner of my mouth.

"My pleasure, boss," replied Peppermint. "Let's just not do that again anytime soon, if you please."

EPILOGUE

It was Christmas Day. Trixie, Ursula, and I had spent the morning opening gifts and enjoying a celebratory Christmas meal together. After the week we'd had, it was a welcome change of pace. At the moment, the two ladies in my life had decided to walk the turkey's tryptophan off and were enjoying a spectacular sixty-two-degree day outside.

I wasn't entirely sure where Peppermint had gotten off to, but I'd decided to give him the day off anyway. He'd earned a much-needed holiday, in my opinion. Besides, it was high time I really thought about his deal with Horatio and just how much longer I could, in good conscience, keep him under the House's "thumb," so to speak. He was a wild spirit, after all. Not suited to service indefinitely—and, I had to admit, he'd done quite well for himself in this recent murder ordeal.

I reflected on his fate while in the kitchen, washing dishes. It wasn't a chore that was necessary. The House, of course, could have taken care of it for me. But there was something about the simple mundane task of washing a dish or a glass that appealed to me right then. It was quiet, allowing my mind to process everything that had happened in recent days.

Eli Smart had been arraigned and had been placed in a psychiatric facility for observation. While he hadn't been insane to think I was the *real* Santa Claus, his actions due to that belief proved that some type of mental break had occurred in the poor boy's mind. Instead of punishment for his crimes, it was my fervent hope that he'd get the help he needed to deal with the loss of his father.

With Mallory O'Hare's permission, I'd given twenty-five thousand dollars of what she'd paid Hank to George so he could recoup some of what he'd lost in the deal with Vinnie Tarturo. The other twenty-five grand had been sent to Teddy Gorshon's ex-wife, to be set up as a college fund for the kids. I wasn't sure why Mallory had been so willing to let me do that with her money. Probably another means of keeping me quiet about her relationship with Trixie. But I didn't care. It was a good deed on her part, whatever her motive, and I wouldn't forget it anytime soon.

There was still the problem of Mallory's secret in regard to Trixie. I'd given my word; I wouldn't tell Trix about her grandmother, but I wouldn't exactly hinder things if she happened to find out on her own. It was, after all, a very small town. And more and more people were discovering her secret. It wouldn't be too long before the girl found out. I doubted it would be a pleasant revelation, and I vowed to do whatever was necessary to help the kid through it when she did.

As for Vinnie Tarturo, a grand jury was currently looking into his business affairs and possible connection with the disappearance of Jose Jimenez. Seems some of the mobster's DNA had been found in Jose's garage, linking him directly to the disappearance. With any luck, Christmas would be without a mafia don in the foreseeable future.

I also now had a better understanding of the House's odd behavior lately. Each time it had "misbehaved," Eli had been in the vicinity. Even the night of Teddy's murder and the appearance of Tinsel had been because of Eli's visit. The House had been trying to tell me who the killer was all along, and I just hadn't caught the clues. It was something I hoped to rectify in the future.

I was drying off the last of the dishes when the House let out an excited groan. I stopped mid-wipe and looked up at the ceiling.

"Seriously?" I asked it. "I thought we were coming to some type of understanding."

Another groan and a rumble under my feet.

I closed my eyes and took a deep breath, focusing on what the House might be trying to tell me now. Honestly, the groan hadn't been worrisome. In fact, if you can attribute an emotion to a structure like a house at all, I could only describe it as "joyful."

Someone the House adored had come for a visit, which meant only one person I could think of.

Placing the last plate into the dish rack, I dried my hands off, slipped into my suit jacket, and glanced up at the ceiling. "See? I'm learning to listen to you better, right?"

GRROOOAAAN.

I smiled at this, then strode from the kitchen into the showroom. As expected, the downstairs was devoid of any guests. That's because the person who'd popped by was currently standing in the one room in the House that only I—and one other—was allowed to enter. The House's heart. Its very soul, if you will.

Straightening my bow tie, I walked over to the nearest wall, which spread itself into a wide doorway for me without even my needing to request it. I entered the passage beyond and weaved my way through the maze with confident, easy strides. As I walked, the walls shifted and changed, creating a new path with every two or three steps I took. I had no idea what direction I was moving in. Had no clue where the "room" was actually located in the House. But then, I didn't need to. I knew without question that the passages would lead me to exactly where I needed to be when the time was right.

Within five minutes, I found myself standing at an old stone door with a wooden latch and large iron hinges. I lifted the latch and watched as the door swung inward, revealing a vast circular stone chamber within.

The room—the place, really—was called *Santheleon*. A world between worlds. A universe in and of itself that connected all other realities—including Wyndter—to our own. The House itself was part of Santheleon. It's what made it sentient. What made it different from all other houses on Earth. But this room in particular—the doorway to Santheleon—was beyond any-thing imaginable. To come here uninvited is to court madness; but thankfully, I had an open invitation whenever the need arose.

I stepped into Santheleon and was instantly greeted by the guttural echoes of manic giggling reverberating through the chamber.

Who has come? said a disembodied high-pitched voice.

A tasty morsel, perhaps? said another.

"You know who I am," I said aloud. "And you know why I've come."

Always takes the fun from us, this one does, said the first voice.

Never lets us eat it, said the second.

The voice, despite having at least two distinct personalities—and potentially millions more—belonged to the N'ahk, the old-est living creature to ever exist. It was said, at one time, that the N'ahk had been a great stag within the Garden of Eden, but I wasn't sure that was true. Like Tinsel the Alligator, I'd never ac-tually seen the being, who was the guardian of Santheleon and protector of the paths to the multitude of dimensions. One thing was clear: the creature was insane. But it wasn't evil. In fact, it represented one of the most benevolent forces in the universe in its capacity with Santheleon. Its little jokes about eating me, I was convinced, were merely its attempt at humor over the ferocity its visage was said to give off.

"I've been summoned here," I said. "I'd like to see *him*, if you please."

Oh, very well, the N'ahk said. *See him, you shall.*

With that, the stone chamber dematerialized around me, and I was suddenly struck with a frigid blast of air. The next moment, I was standing in a cozy little room. The walls were made of timber and there was a roaring fire burning on an immense stone hearth. Stockings hung from the mantel over the fire; but, from what I could tell, there were no gifts, oranges, or coal in any of them.

To my left was a window. Beyond that was a landscape painted in white and blue. Mountains sprouted up in the distance, and I could just make out the setting sun over the ridge of one of them.

A robust chuckle came from behind me. I wheeled around to see a giant of a man. Not quite as tall as me, but big. Muscular. Wearing a leather tunic and a wide belt adorned with an enormous brass buckle. The man's forearms were bare and massive, the size of a lumberjack's. A gold-hilted Roman-era sword hung from the man's hip as he beamed at me behind a thick gray—not white, mind you—mane of hair. His equally gray beard was a patchwork mess, made even more remarkable by the eight-inch scar down his right cheek.

"Krin'Ghal!" I said, returning his smile. "It's great to see you again."

"Same to you, Thomas. I'm very pleased with the outcome

of that horrible affair with Mr. Cobb. I'm saddened, of course, about Eli. But I'll look after him while he gets the treatment he needs."

"Thank you. I appreciate that."

For a moment the two of us stood there staring at each other. I shifted from one foot to the other, waiting for him to broach the subject of this unexpected visit. I doubted it was simply a desire to congratulate me on solving a murder. Such things tend to go over the Spirit of Christmas's head. So, I waited for him to speak.

But he didn't.

I waited some more. I cleared my throat, hoping to egg him on.

Then someone else cleared their throat, and I tensed. Someone was standing behind the Krin'Ghal who I hadn't been aware of. I tried to peer around the giant's enormous form but couldn't see who it was. I glanced up into Santa's twinkling eyes, but he merely stared back at me.

"Um, Krin'Ghal," I said. "Mind introducing me to your friend back there? I didn't know we had company."

The big man chuckled at this. He did so enjoy his little games, and for some reason he was particularly beside himself with pride over this one.

"Certainly," he said, although he didn't move out of the way. "But first understand something. The time of my ascension is quickly approaching. This old body cries out for the tranquility of the Great Reward. Your time will come soon, so although I'd like you to listen to this man—to assist him, if you can—just know that your time among the mortals is drawing to a close." He paused, a twinkle in his eye as he beamed. "Now, Thomas, don't say no right away. Give him a chance to explain."

That last bit was rather ominous, but Krin'Ghal stepped aside before I could question him about it. Once he moved, I saw a handsome dark-haired man, wearing a black three-piece suit with a black button-down shirt and black tie. He smiled at me, his teeth radiantly white, which nearly kept me blinded to the pencil-thin Errol Flynn moustache just under his nose.

My heart sank at the sight of him, and I took a step back. I knew who this was.

The man in black clapped his hands together dramatically, and he spun around in a pirouette when he observed the recognition on my face. He laughed. It was both melodious and childlike. A complete incongruity for the being I knew him to be.

"Allow me to introduce myself," the man said, reaching out an immaculately manicured hand. "My name is Silas Mot. The Grim Reaper. And after the little murder investigation you just pulled off, I could use your help with a little problem I've been having with a rather unusual case."

AFTERWORD

Now that you've finished the book, there are a few things you may be scratching your head about. (I hope the head-scratching isn't from the mystery itself, though!)

I am, of course, referring to the numerous references throughout the book regarding Krin'Ghal (the original Santa carried a sword?!), Santheleon, and the strange and mysterious N'ahk. You might be thinking you're quite the expert on folklore concerning Kris Kringle, and you may well be right, because nothing in world mythology refers to any of these things. They are creations of my own and are found only in my 2014 fantasy novel *The Legend of the Winterking: The Crown of Nandur*, which set out to explore the origins of the legend behind Kringle from my own little corner of the imagination.

In the book, the "original" Santa was an orphan boy named Krin, raised by the Bishop of Myra (modern-day Turkey), Nicholas (who was also a member of the Order of the Magi—yes, the same Magi that visited Christ when he was about two years old). As the story progresses, Krin discovers that he is half human and half elf, and heir to the realm of Wyndter, another dimension that resides parallel to our own world and is inhabited by dark creatures known as the Fae. *The Legend of the Winterking* was intended to be a trilogy that explored Krin's overthrow of the fierce Krampus, one of the biblical Nephilim that usurped Krin's father and took over Wyndter with an iron fist and a desire to enter our world and subjugate it to his rule as well.

Unfortunately, Book One just didn't sell well enough to warrant the amount of work it would take to finish the trilogy, and the story drifted into obscurity (albeit always in the back of my mind to perhaps one day return to it). While *The Knives Before Christmas* is vastly different from *The Legend of the Winterking*, I thought it only fair to include, in this book, the mythology I had created. Not only was it fun for me, but I hope it makes some of Krin's fans happy to see that his influence is still alive and well in my fictional worlds.

The final head-scratcher in the book you might be wondering about occurred in the Epilogue, with the introduction to the black-suited and debonaire Silas Mot. If you're not sure who he is, you should check out my Grim Days Mysteries series, in which the Grim Reaper himself comes to a small Florida town to solve a series of wild, unusual deaths that he didn't sanction. And who knows...if all goes well with this book, maybe we'll see a full-fledged team-up between the two in a future book!

As always, if you enjoyed this book, spread the word! And I'd certainly appreciate your leaving a review. It helps get the book in readers' hands and ensures that more books in this series will get written. And who knows: if there's a strong enough clamor for it, we just might see *The Legend of the Winterking* burst back onto the publishing scene! I hope so, anyway!

ABOUT THE AUTHOR

Bestselling author **J. KENT HOLLOWAY** lives on death. Literally. With more than twenty-seven years' experience in forensic death investigations, he's seen it all. Experienced the worst that life has to give and never let it dim his sense of wonder or humor. Now, he brings all this experience, along with a zeal for uncovering the folklore and superstitions of death, to the written page as author of mysteries and forensic crime fiction. He is the author of the fun, breezy Grim Days Mystery series, as well as the critically acclaimed Ezekiel Crane paranormal mystery series. He's also the author of the Cold War era tropical island/voodoo/KGB-packed calypso-inspired mystery, *Killypso Island* and the forensic thriller, *Clean Exit*.

Kent Holloway also has a master's degree in biblical studies from Southeastern Baptist Theological Seminary. He has served as singles minister, evangelism pastor, and director of discipleship and education. In 2019, Kent released his very first Christian nonfiction book entitled *I Died Swallowing a Goldfish and Other Life Lessons from the Morgue* that features tales of his real-life investigations with the important lessons he's learned from them. He currently resides in Florida.

www.ingramcontent.com/pod-product-compliance
Lightning Source LLC
Chambersburg PA
CBHW030328030726
47499CB00003B/687